GUSTAV GLOOM

AND THE PEOPLE TAKER

GUSTAV GLOOM
AND THE PEOPLE TAKER

by Adam-Troy Castro
illustrated by Kristen Margiotta

SCHOLASTIC INC.

ISBN 978-0-545-62187-8

12 11 10 9 8 7 6 5 4 3 2 1   13 14 15 16 17 18/0

Printed in the U.S.A.   40

First Scholastic printing, October 2013

Book design by Christina Quintero

Typeset in MrsEaves, Neutraface, and Strangelove Text

This one's for Harlan Ellison,

friend,

teacher,

inspiration,

and keeper of the gates of fantasy

CHAPTER ONE
THE STRANGE FATE OF MR. NOTES

The neighbors thought Gustav Gloom was the unhappiest little boy in the world.

None of them bothered to talk to him to see if there was anything they could do to make his life better. That would be "getting involved." But they could look, and as far as they could see, he always wore his mouth in a frown, he always stuck his lower lip out as if about to burst into tears, and he always dressed in a black suit with a black tie as if about to go to a funeral or just wanting to be prepared in case one broke out without warning.

Gustav's skin was pale, and he always had dark circles under his eyes as if he hadn't had enough sleep. A little quirk of his eyelids kept them half closed all the time, making him look like he wasn't paying attention. His shiny black hair stood straight up, like tar-covered grass.

Everybody who lived on Sunnyside Terrace said, "Somebody ought to do something about that sad little boy."

Of course, when they said *somebody* ought to do something, they really meant *somebody else*.

Nobody wanted to end up like poor Mr. Notes from the Neighborhood Standards Committee.

Mr. Notes had worked for the little town where they all lived. His job was making sure people took care of their neighborhoods, and the neighbors on Sunnyside Terrace had asked him to visit the Gloom house because it didn't fit the rest of the neighborhood at all.

All of the other houses on Sunnyside Terrace were lime green, peach pink, or strawberry red. Each front yard had one bush and one tree, the bush next to the front door and the tree right up against the street. Anybody who decided to live on the street had to sign special contracts promising that they wouldn't "ruin" the "character" of the "community" by putting up "unauthorized trees" or painting their front doors "unauthorized colors," and so on.

The old, dark house where Gustav Gloom lived had been built long before the others, long before there was a neighborhood full of rules.

It was a big black mansion, more like a castle than a proper house. There were four looming towers, one at every corner, each of them ringed by stone gargoyles wearing expressions that suggested they'd just tasted something bad. There were no windows on the ground floor, just a set of double doors twice as tall as the average man. The windows on the upper floors were all black rectangles that might have been glass covered with paint or clear glass looking into absolute darkness.

Though this was already an awful lot of black for one house, even the lawn surrounding the place was black, with all-black flowers and a single black tree with no leaves. There was also a grayish-black fog that always covered the ground to ankle height, dissolving into wisps wherever it passed between the iron bars of the fence.

The lone tree looked like a skeletal hand clawing its way out of the ground. It was home to ravens who seemed to regard the rest of the neighborhood with as much offense as the rest of the neighborhood regarded the Gloom house. The ravens said *caw* pretty much all day.

The neighbors didn't like the ravens.

They said, "Somebody ought to do something about those ravens."

They didn't like the house.

They said, "Somebody ought to do something about that house."

They didn't like the whole situation, really.

They said, "Somebody ought to do something about those people, with their strange house and their big ugly tree that looks like a hand and their little boy with the strange black hair."

They called the mayor's office to complain. And the mayor's office didn't know what to do about it, so they called the City Planning Commission. And the City Planning Commission called Mr. Notes, who was away on his first vacation in four years but whom they made a point of bothering because nobody liked him.

They asked Mr. Notes, "Will you please come back and visit the people in this house and ask them to paint their house some other color?"

And poor Mr. Notes, who was on a road trip traveling to small towns all over the country taking pictures of his one interest in life, antique weather vanes shaped like roosters, had folded his road map and sighed. "Well, if I *have* to."

4

On the morning Mr. Notes pulled up to the curb, five-year-old Gustav Gloom sat on a swing hanging from the big black tree, reading a big black book.

Mr. Notes was not happy about having to walk past the boy to get to the house because he didn't like little boys very much. He didn't like little girls very much, either. Or, for that matter, most adults. Mr. Notes liked houses, especially if they matched the rest of their neighborhoods and had great weather vanes shaped like roosters.

Mr. Notes was so tall and so skinny that his legs looked like sticks. His knees and elbows bulged like marbles beneath his pin-striped, powder-blue suit. He wore a flat straw hat with a daisy in the band and had a mustache that looked like somebody had glued paintbrush bristles under his nose.

He opened the iron gate, expecting it to groan at him the way most old iron gates do, but it made no sound at all, not even when he slammed it shut behind him. He might have been bothered by the lack of any *clang*, but was even more upset by the odd coldness of the air inside the gate. When he looked up, he saw a big, dark rain cloud overhead, keeping any direct sunlight from touching the property.

He did not think that maybe he should turn around and get back in his car. He just turned to the strange little boy on the swing and said, "Excuse me? Little boy?"

Gustav looked up from the big fat book he was reading, which, like his house, his clothes, and even his tree, was all black. Even the pages. It looked like too heavy a book for a little boy to even hold, let alone read. He said, "Yes?"

Some conversations are like leaky motorboats, running out of fuel before you even leave the dock. This, Mr. Notes began to sense, was one of them. He ran through his limited collection of appropriate things to say to children and found only one thing, a question that he threw out with the desperation of a man terrified of dogs who tosses a ball in the hope that they'll run away to fetch it: "Are your mommy and daddy home?"

Gustav blinked at him. "No."

"Is—"

"Or," Gustav said, "really, they might be home, wherever their home is, but they're not *here*."

"Excuse me, young man, but this is very *serious*.

I don't have time to *play games*. Is there anyone inside that house I can *talk to*?"

Gustav blinked at him again. "Oh, sure."

Mr. Notes brushed his stiff mustache with the tip of a finger and turned his attention to the house itself, which if anything looked even bigger and darker and more like a giant looming shadow than it had before.

As he watched, the front doors swung inward, revealing a single narrow hallway with a shiny wooden floor and a red carpet marking a straight path all the way from the front door to a narrower opening in the far wall.

Whatever lay beyond that farther doorway was too dark to see.

Mr. Notes sniffed at Gustav. "I'm going to tell your family how *rude* you were."

Gustav said, "Why would you tell them that when it isn't true?"

"I know rudeness when I see it."

"You must not have ever seen it, then," Gustav said, "because that's not what I was."

Mr. Notes could not believe the nerve of the little boy, who had dared to suggest that there was any problem with his manners. What he planned to say to the people inside would ruin the boy's whole day.

He turned his back on the little boy and stormed up the path into the house, getting almost all the way down the corridor before the big black doors closed behind him.

Nobody on Sunnyside Terrace ever figured out what happened during Mr. Notes's seventeen minutes in the Gloom mansion before the doors opened again and he came running out, yelling at the top of his lungs and moving as fast as his long, spindly legs could carry him.

He ran down the front walk and out the gate and past his car and around the bend and out of sight, never to be seen again on Sunnyside Terrace.

When he finally stopped, he was too busy screaming at the top of his lungs to make any sense. What the neighbors took from it, by the time he was done, was that going anywhere near the Gloom house had been a very bad idea, and that having it "ruin" the "character" of the neighborhood was just the price they'd have to pay for not having to go anywhere near the house themselves.

Mr. Notes was sent to a nice, clean home for very nervous people and remains there to this day, making pot holders out of yarn and ashtrays out of clay and drawings of black circles with black crayons. By happy coincidence, his private room looks out upon the roof and offers him a fine view of the building's weather vane, which looks like a rooster. It's fair to say that he's gotten what he always wanted.

But one strange thing still puzzles the doctors and the nurses at the special home for people who once had a really bad scare and can't get over it.

It's the one symptom of his condition that they can't find in any of their medical books and that they can't explain no matter how many times they ask him to open his mouth and say *ah*, the one thing that makes them shudder whenever they see all his drawings of a big black shape that looks like an open mouth.

It was the main reason that all the neighbors on Sunnyside Terrace, who still said that "somebody" had to do something about the Gloom house, now left it alone and pretended that it had nothing to do with them.

And that was this: No matter how bright it is around him, wherever he happens to be, Mr. Notes no longer casts a shadow.

CHAPTER TWO
THE ARRIVAL OF FERNIE WHAT

Like always, Mr. What was careful to make sure his daughters weren't worried.

He said, "Don't worry, girls."

Neither ten-year-old Fernie nor her twelve-year-old sister, Pearlie, who were riding in the backseat while their dad drove to the family's new home on Sunnyside Terrace, had said anything at all about being worried.

They rarely said anything of the sort.

But their dad had always been under the impression that they were frightened little things who spent their lives one moment away from panic and were only kept calm by his constant reassurances that everything was going to be all right.

He thought this even though they took after their mother, who had never been scared of anything and was currently climbing the

Matterhorn or something. She was a professional adventurer. She made TV programs that featured her doing impossibly dangerous things like tracking abominable snowmen and parachuting off waterfalls.

"I know it looks like I made a wrong turn," he said, regarding the perfectly calm and sunny neighborhood around them as if giant people-eating monsters crouched hidden behind every house, "but there's no reason for alarm. I should be able to turn around and get back on the map any second now."

The What girls, who looked like versions of each other down to their freckled cheeks and fiery red hair, had spent so much of their lives listening to their father's warnings about scary things happening that they could have grown up in two different ways: as scared of everything as he was, or so tired of being told to be scared that they sought out scary things on general principle the way their mother did.

The second way was more fun. Right now, Fernie was reading a book about monsters who lived in an old, dark house and took unwary kids down into its basement to make them work in an evil robot factory, and Pearlie was playing a handheld video game about aliens who come to this planet to gobble up entire cities.

The final member of the family, Harrington, wasn't worried, either. He was a four-year-old black-and-white cat enjoying happy cat dreams in his cat carrier. Those dreams had to do with a tinier version of Mr. What making high-pitched squeaks as Harrington batted at him with a paw.

"Uh-oh," Mr. What said. And then, quickly, "It's no real problem. I just missed the turnoff. I hope I don't run out of gas; we only have three quarters of a tank left."

Mr. What was a professional worrier. Companies hired him to look around their offices and find all the horrible hidden dangers that could be prepared for by padding corners and putting up warning signs. If you've ever been in a building and seen a safety railing where no safety railing needs to be, just standing there in the middle of the floor all by itself as if it is the only thing that keeps anybody from tripping over their own feet, then you've probably seen a place where Mr. What has been.

Mr. What knew the hidden dangers behind every object in the entire world. It didn't matter what it was; he knew a tragic accident that involved one. In Mr. What's world, people were always poking their eyes out with mattress tags and drowning in pudding cups.

If people listened to everything he said, they would have spent their entire lives hiding in their beds with their blankets up over their heads.

Mr. What switched on the left-turn signal and explained, "Don't worry, girls. I'm just making a left turn."

Pearlie jabbed her handheld video game, sending another ugly alien to its bloody doom. "That's a relief, Dad."

"Don't hold that thing too close to your face," he warned. "It gives off lots of radiation, and the last thing you want is a fried brain."

Fernie said, "Gee, Dad, can we have that for dinner tonight?"

"Have what?" he asked, jumping a little as the car behind him beeped in protest at him for going twenty miles an hour under the speed limit.

"A fried brain. That sounds delicious."

Pearlie said, "That sounds disgusting."

Coming from her, that wasn't a complaint. It was a compliment.

Mr. What said, "That was very mean of you,

Fernie. You'll give your sister nightmares by saying things like that."

Pearlie hadn't suffered a nightmare since she was six.

"And Fernie, don't make a face at your sister," Mr. What continued, somehow aware that Fernie had crossed her eyes, twisted her lips, and stuck her tongue out the side of her mouth. "You'll stick that way."

Mr. What had written a book of documented stories about little girls who had made twisted faces only to then trip over an untied shoelace or something, causing their faces to stick that way for the rest of their lives, which must have made it difficult for them to ever have a social life, get a job, or be taken seriously.

Fernie and Pearlie had once spent a long afternoon testing the theory, each one taking turns crossing her eyes, sticking out her tongue, and stretching her mouth in weird ways while the other slapped her on the back at the most grotesque possible moments.

They'd both been disappointed when it hadn't worked.

Mr. What said, "Hey, we can see our new house from here!"

Both girls saw the big black house behind the big black gates and started shouting in excitement: Fernie, because she loved the idea of living in a haunted house, and Pearlie because she loved the idea of living in any house that was black and mysterious, whether it was haunted or not.

Mr. What naturally assumed that the girls were screaming in terror instead of enthusiasm. "Don't worry," he said as he pulled into the driveway directly across the street. "It's not *that* one. It's this one, here."

Now that the girls saw which house their father had really been talking about, they gaped in scandalized horror. "What *color* is that?"

"Fluorescent Salmon," said Mr. What.

The little house did indeed look like the fish when it's put on a plate to eat, only more sparkly, which might be perfectly fine inside a fish, but not so good, as far as the girls were concerned, on a house.

Fluorescent Salmon, it turned out, was just the right color to give Fernie What a pounding headache. "I'd rather live in the scary house."

Mr. What looked at the big black house as if seeing it for the first time. "That broken-down old place? I'm sure all the rooms are filled with spiderwebs, all the boards in the floors have pointy nails sticking out of them, and the staircases have plenty of broken steps that will collapse under your weight and leave you hanging for your life by your fingernails."

Both girls cried, "Cool!"

Gustav Gloom stood behind the iron fence of the Gloom mansion, watching the new neighbors emerge from their car. His mouth was a thin black line, his eyes a pair of sad, white marbles. Standing behind the long black bars—and going unnoticed by the girls, for the moment—he looked a little like a prisoner begging to be let out.

He had grown quite a bit since the day five years earlier when Mr. Notes came to call. He was skinny, but not starved; pale as a sheet of blank paper, but not sickly; serious, but not grim. He still wore a plain black suit with a black tie, and his black hair still stood straight up like a lawn that hadn't been mowed recently.

He still looked like the unhappiest little boy in the world, only older.

The What family can be forgiven for not seeing him right away, in part because they were busy dealing with the business of moving into their new house, and in part because it was pretty hard to see Gustav in his black suit standing on his black lawn under the overcast sky over the Gloom residence.

It was just like the big black book Gustav still carried around wherever he went. Most people can't read black ink on black paper. Seeing Gustav could be just as difficult, even on a sunny day when the whites of his eyes stood out like Ping-Pong balls floating in a puddle of ink.

An odd black smoke billowed at his feet. It moved against the wind, and sometimes, when it got enough of itself bunched up around his ankles, his legs seemed to turn transparent and fade into nothingness just below the knees. It was a little like he was standing on the lawn and in an invisible hole at the same time.

There were other patches of blackness darting around the big black lawn, some of them large and some of them small—all of them hard to see against the ebony grass. But all of them seemed as interested as Gustav Gloom in the doings across the street.

One of those dark shapes left the black house and slid across the black grass, stopping only when it found Gustav watching the two What girls and their incredibly nervous father unload cardboard boxes from the trunk of their car.

To both Gustav and the shape that now rose from the ground, the girls were bright in ways that had nothing to do with how smart they were. They were bright in the way they captured the light of the sun and seemed to double it before giving it back to the world.

The shape watched, along with Gustav Gloom, as the littler of the two girls carried her box of books into the new house.

"Those are scary books," the shape said. "I can tell from here. And from the way they all smell like her, that little girl must have read some of them half a dozen times. She likes spooky things, that one. A girl like that, who enjoys being scared, she's not going to be kept away from a house like this, no matter how stern the warning. I wager she'll be over here for a visit and making friends with you before that cat of hers takes its first stop at its litter pan."

Gustav gave the black shape a nod; as always, he offered no smile, but the *sense* of a smile, the easy affection that comes only after years of trust.

"Why not hope for the best, just this once?" the shape asked. "Why can't you believe me when I say that she'll be over here saying hello before the day is out?"

Gustav looked away from the view on the other side of the gate and gave one of his most serious looks to the black shape beside him: the shape of a man so tall and so skinny that his legs looked like sticks, with knees and elbows that bulged like marbles beneath the shape (but not color) of a pin-striped, powder-blue suit.

It was not Mr. Notes, who plays no further role in this story, and who we can safely assume continued to live in the home for nervous people and use up little boxes of black crayons for the rest of his days.

It had the outline of Mr. Notes and the manner of Mr. Notes and even the voice of Mr. Notes, except that it didn't sound like it was breathing through its nose like Mr. Notes did, and its words didn't come with that little extra added tone that Mr. Notes had used to give the impression that everything around him smelled bad.

It was the part of Mr. Notes that had stayed behind when Mr. Notes ran screaming from the Gloom house, a part that he would not have wanted to leave behind, but a part that had not liked Mr. Notes very much and had therefore abandoned him, anyway.

Its decision to remain behind was the main reason the real Mr. Notes now had to live in a padded room.

"Don't worry," the shadow of Mr. Notes said. "You'll be friends soon enough."

Gustav thought about the girls, who seemed to have been born to live in sunlight, and for just a second or two, he became exactly what he'd always seemed to be to all the neighbors on Sunnyside Terrace: the saddest little boy in the world.

"I have to warn her," he said.

CHAPTER THREE
THE ODD TALE OF MRS. ADELE EVERWINER AND THE RUDE CASHIER

To Fernie What's infinite disappointment, the salmon-colored house contained no spiderwebs or boards with pointy nails sticking up. Nor was there any stairway with or without weak steps that might collapse without warning and leave the girls hanging for their lives over the basement.

In fact, there wasn't a basement of any size, or for that matter an attic, and as everybody knows, no house can be at all interesting unless it has either an attic or a basement for the storage of dusty and possibly dangerous things.

There wasn't even any furniture to climb on, not yet; just a bunch of empty rooms with nothing in them but the sunbeams streaming in through the windows.

It wasn't that Fernie *actually* wanted her new house to be secretly inhabited by monsters. She preferred her homes monster-free, thank you. But as far as she was concerned, a house that doesn't even have a dark place where monsters *could be* is also a house with no room for secretly pretending that there really are some. What was the fun of that?

Disappointed, Fernie picked a room at random and dropped off Harrington's cat carrier, setting up his food and litter box in a nearby corner.

Harrington took only one step outside his cage before retreating to the safety of imprisonment. This new place didn't smell like him. This was a major problem, since as far as he was concerned, the most important attribute any place could ever have was a nice Harrington smell.

Sounding just like her dad, Fernie said, "Don't worry. It's okay. You'll get used to it."

Had she understood Cat, Fernie would have known that his answering meow didn't mean "I'm not so sure about that, Fernie" as she presumed, but the much more alarming "None of us is going to live long enough for me to get used to it!"

Instead, she petted him once, then went outside to see what was keeping her father, and found him and Pearlie in front of the house talking to a neighbor who had stopped by to give them a warning in Human Being.

Mrs. Adele Everwiner (for that was her name) looked like a human teardrop: wide and rounded at the bottom, narrower at the shoulders, and coming to a point on top. Her hair was as red as an apple and was the part that came to a point, even if the point was a little off center and leaned to the right, as if signaling to drivers behind her that she was about to make a sudden turn into their lane. She had bright-green eyes behind bright-green eye shadow and a nose so small that it looked like it had been placed on her face as an afterthought.

She held a rhinestone-studded leash leading to a little white dog that walked in constant circles without looking at anyone. It was one of the ugliest dogs Fernie had ever seen, as it was missing so many teeth that its tongue lolled out the side of its mouth like a treat it had picked up and forgotten to chew. Mostly it just followed its own shadow around as if expecting it to run away into the bushes as soon as it could.

According to Mrs. Everwiner, the dog's name was Snooks.

"It's actually my fourth dog named Snooks," she explained, in a voice like air escaping from a balloon and wishing it hadn't. "I had one named Snooks and then one named Snooks 2 and then one named Snooks 3. Like I said, this one's my fourth. Can either of you little girls guess his full name?"

"Snooks 4?" Fernie guessed.

"No, Snooks 5. I decided to skip Snooks 4 because Snooks 3 was such a good dog that I didn't want this sweet baby here to start his life at such a disadvantage."

"That was a good idea," Fernie said. "Having too much to live up to can ruin a dog's life."

Pearlie suggested, "You can always have Snooks 4 later on. Once the pressure's off."

"Not a bad idea. As it is," Mrs. Everwiner said, looking down at her dog with an odd mixture of affection and disdain, "he's a strange little dog, frightened of almost everything. I think it's because of *that house*."

She looked around as if frightened of being overheard, then leaned in so close that Fernie could see the little hairs on the tip of her chin.

"Look at that place! I wouldn't want you girls to take this the *wrong way*, but you know how some places don't really belong in the world? How they have secrets that should stay hidden?"

Even though she was reading a book about a haunted house and had a good idea what Mrs. Everwiner was trying to say, Fernie thought it wiser to feign ignorance. "Ummm. No, not really."

"Well," Mrs. Everwiner said, now leaning so close to Fernie that if she were leaning any closer she might have been behind her. "That house over there, it's a bad place. You can tell because the sun never shines on it, and because the birds never fly over it. Just look at it! How can a place that looks like that not be a *bad place*?"

Fernie looked at the house and saw a sad and strange little boy in the front yard, watching her through the iron fence. The idea of that boy having to stand there in his front yard watching Mrs. Everwiner tell people that his house was evil struck her as so unfair that she almost said something rude. "What's so evil about it?"

"By the time you found out," Mrs. Everwiner said, "it would be . . . *too late*."

This was the kind of thing that people say only

in scary movies and only at night and only when they expect thunder to crash right outside the window like an exclamation point. But this was a warm, sunny day, the only cloud was the one that shaded the big dark house, and no thunder obliged.

"We keep asking the city to tear it down," Mrs. Everwiner continued. "Unfortunately, they keep saying they have no *cause*. How can they have no cause? Just look at the place!"

The Whats looked at the place.

Their lack of an immediate response made Mrs. Everwiner change the subject. "By the way, I saw you bring a pet carrier into the house. I hope that was another little dog. Snooks here can always use a friend for playdates."

This, at least, was something that could be answered. "I'm sorry," Mr. What said. "Harrington's a cat."

"Oh," Mrs. Everwiner said. There were several seconds of uncomfortable silence. Apparently she didn't like cats much and ran out of words as soon as one was mentioned. "You don't let it run around loose, do you? You don't really want him to get into a fight with Snooks."

Fernie regarded Snooks (who had just jumped away from his own shadow as if it had turned around and tried to bite him) and found it hard to believe that any fight between Snooks and Harrington would ever happen. "No," she said. "I don't want him to get into a fight with Snooks."

"That's good," Mrs. Everwiner said, "because Snooks is a very high-strung dog and would be so upset if that ever happened that he probably wouldn't eat or poop right for weeks."

"Well," Mr. What said politely, "we wouldn't want Snooks to have any trouble pooping."

"Yes," Fernie said. "We were worried about that when we drove in."

Mr. What began to tell Mrs. Everwiner about all the special precautions he was going to take to make sure Harrington didn't get out of the house and bother Snooks, and he was so busy detailing the procedures that he missed seeing what Fernie saw.

Snooks had scrambled away from his shadow as if it had tried to bite him a second time. In fact, Fernie realized with a start, it *had* tried to bite him. The shadow was running around the actual dog in circles, sniffing his rear end and nipping at his tail. Snooks was so disturbed by all the shadow's attentions that he whined and walked in circles and looked up at Mrs. Everwiner, begging her with his big brown eyes to notice how badly he was being bullied. But Mrs. Everwiner was too busy to notice, as she was too involved with telling Mr. What more about her dog's nervous conditions, which, in addition to being scared of the house across the street, also included being angry at the toilet bowl and in love with the umbrella stand.

Fernie wanted to say, "Yes, that's all very interesting, but if you'll just look down you'll see something even weirder: your dog's shadow picking a fight with him." But all that came out was a little amazed squeak. Unable to come up with any way to get her family's attention other than just opening her eyes as wide as possible, Fernie could only watch as the shadow dog grew tired of baiting the real dog and ran across the street.

Then she saw the second impossible thing she'd seen in about as many seconds: Snooks's runaway shadow leaped between the iron bars in the fence and into the sad little boy's arms, licking his face with doggy affection.

Fernie whirled toward her father, hoping against hope that he'd seen it, too. But, no; Mr. What was too busy listening to Mrs. Everwiner, who had changed the subject and was now going on at great length about a local supermarket with a cashier that had been rude to her and why this meant Mr. What should never shop there.

Even Pearlie paid close attention to this, not because it was the most fascinating subject in the world but because she was fascinated that anybody would ever think it was.

Feeling a little like her body was a car and she'd just been handed the steering wheel without knowing how to drive, Fernie murmured "Excuse me" and slipped away somewhere during Mrs. Everwiner's breathless story about giving that rude cashier a piece of her mind.

Nobody noticed her crossing the street, not even when Mrs. Everwiner had gone on to the part of the story about demanding to see the rude cashier's manager and that manager getting the same piece of her mind, only louder.

Nobody stopped Fernie from approaching the place in the iron fence closest to the sad-looking little boy, who stood holding a black book in one hand and the smoky, gray shadow of the little dog in the other.

Behind her, Mrs. Everwiner had gone on to explain how the manager's apology had failed to satisfy her, and how she'd demanded a personal phone call from the company headquarters in St. Louis. But ahead of her, the sad little boy stood ankle-deep in gray mist.

To Fernie, it was a lot like being in a dream, but she had always been polite, even in dreams, so she found herself saying, "Hello. I'm Fernie What. Like in the question."

"What question?"

"Like in any question that starts with *what*. My first name is Fernie and my last name is What. When I say 'My name is Fernie What,' many people say 'Fernie what?' again, like a question, so I kind of have to beat them to it by saying, 'Like in the question.'"

The sad little boy nodded. "I can see how that would happen. But I got it the first time. I'm Gustav Gloom."

"That's a strange name."

"So's Fernie What."

He had a good point, of course, but all of this was dancing around the real reason she had come across the street, the thing she now found she was having a little trouble coming out and actually saying. "You're playing with Snooks's shadow."

"Yes," Gustav Gloom said as Snooks's shadow licked him on the cheek. "It's much nicer than the actual dog."

Fernie resisted a strange need to stamp her foot. "But that can't be."

"Sure it can," Gustav Gloom said. "The real dog bites." When he put the shadow dog down, it ran around him three times, panting in canine joy, before slipping back through the fence and galloping across the street to the flesh-and-blood Snooks, who did not seem all that happy that it had returned.

Mrs. Everwiner had just gotten to the part of the story about the angry letter she'd written to the newspaper, whose editors were so horrified that a woman of her station would ever have an unsatisfactory experience in a supermarket that they put her letter on the front page beneath a giant headline of the kind most newspapers reserve for warnings about erupting volcanoes. It was even bigger, Mrs. Everwiner proudly assured them, than the headline over the latest story about all those mysterious disappearances that had plagued the town over the past few months: Seven people so far, some plucked from their beds, had all disappeared without a trace.

Fernie's father and sister, who were still trapped listening to Mrs. Everwiner's story, hadn't noticed the departure and return of the dog's shadow any more than they'd noticed the absence of Fernie. This was distinctly odd, as Fernie's father always noticed when his daughters crossed streets, in part because he knew that even the most quiet streets could without warning become runways for airplanes coming in for emergency landings. For as long as Fernie could remember, he'd always watched his daughters carefully to make sure that they didn't cross any street without looking not only left and right but also up.

But Fernie couldn't let go of the one thing she'd seen that was distinctly odder. "Shadow dogs don't just walk away from their real dogs."

"It happens all the time," Gustav said.

"You're crazy."

"You saw it happen," Gustav pointed out.

"But it doesn't happen *all the time!*"

"If it happens once," Gustav said, "it can happen more than once. And if it can happen more than once, it can happen all the time. It's not my fault that you've never noticed it before."

"I'm surprised enough that it happened even once."

Gustav shrugged. "So now you've seen it happen once and you don't have to be surprised the next time it happens."

Again, Fernie wanted to stamp her foot. "But that doesn't explain anything! Shadows can't run around by themselves!"

"Who says they can't?"

The simple question nearly swept Fernie's legs out from under her. Because as it turned out, she didn't have an answer. She couldn't remember anybody in her life ever telling her what a shadow could or could not do; not even her father, who knew fourteen ways television sets could explode if you changed channels too quickly. No, she realized now, her general understanding of the things a shadow could or could not do had just come into being all by itself. Even so, it still hurt her head to think about. "Even mine?"

"Why not?"

"Because it's a shadow! It does what I do!"

"You haven't been watching it carefully enough."

"I could watch it all day!" Fernie cried. "It would still only do what I do! That's what a shadow is!"

"Then," Gustav said, "explain the dog."

Across the street, Mrs. Everwiner had reached the part of her epic story where the local TV station got involved, devoting the longest segment of the nightly news to her complaint about the cashier, preempting the story about all the missing people entirely.

The repercussions of Mrs. Everwiner's one moment of inconvenience at the supermarket just seemed to keep expanding outward, like a stubborn weed intent on overgrowing the entire world. At this rate, Fernie would not have been surprised to find out that wars had been fought over it.

Pearlie and their dad still feigned interest, unaware that Fernie was involved in a much more interesting conversation just across the street. As much as Fernie wanted to resolve the confusion over what shadows could or could not do, she found herself needing to get back to them, if only for a moment, just to make sure she could return to a world that made sense.

"Go ahead," Gustav Gloom said, sounding

sadder than ever. "Leave. I can tell you want to."

Fernie felt terrible. "Don't take it personally. I'm just busy moving in. We have lots of boxes to take in."

"I'm sure you do," said Gustav Gloom. "And I'm sure that you'll be warned not to come over here ever again, because this house is a *bad place* and there's nothing but trouble for you here."

"Is that true?"

"It's what people will say. And they'll also say to stay away from me, because I live here and that makes me as bad as the house."

Fernie felt worse with every word the strange little boy spoke. "Well, if the house is the problem, why do we have to talk here? Why can't you come across the street with me and meet my family?"

Gustav Gloom looked at Fernie and flashed one of the oddest expressions Fernie had ever seen: not sadness, but not happiness, either. It struck her as the look a person gets when he knows a joke that's funny only to him. "I'm sorry. I can't leave my yard."

Something about the way he said it made his meaning clear: It wasn't a case of being forbidden from leaving his yard by parents who'd promised to punish him if he did; it was a case of being unable to leave, of being confined by the fence and the clouds that cast a shadow over his house like an animal inside a cage.

Fernie's mouth hung open. "Are you locked in there?"

"No."

"Then why can't you leave?"

"I just can't, that's all."

"Why can't you?"

He struggled to come up with the words. "It's . . . the only place I can *be*."

"What happens if you try to leave?"

"I'm not sure I can explain."

"Don't you go to school?"

"No."

"Never even been to anybody else's house?"

"No."

Fernie blinked. "That's sad."

Gustav Gloom said, "I know."

"Do you have anybody in there to keep you company?"

"Nobody with bodies."

Fernie wasn't sure she'd heard him correctly. "What?"

"Most of them ignore me, but some are

family, sort of. It's okay as long as I stay away from the bad places."

"What bad places?"

"The *bad* places," he repeated as if that explained everything. And then, after a moment's thought, he added, "You need to be careful, too. It isn't always safe even on your side of the fence. The People Taker goes out hunting at night."

"What do you mean?"

Instead of answering, he cocked his head like a puppy hearing a whistle from far, far away. "I'm sorry. I'm being called. It was nice to meet you, Fernie What. Maybe I'll see you again."

And then he walked away.

But there was also something very strange about the way he walked away, something about the way the gray mist at his ankles bubbled up around him with every step, the way the air seemed to thicken and turn black the farther he went, until it was hard to make out his black hair and black suit against the darkness that surrounded him even in daylight.

CHAPTER FOUR
HARRINGTON THE CAT MAKES AN ENEMY

That night Fernie enjoyed one of her favorite dreams: the one about the atomic zombies.

In this dream she was the last girl in the shattered ruins of a once-great city, fighting zombies who were not just zombies, because that had gotten boring after the first four or five times she had the dream, but *atomic* zombies, who had gotten too close to a glowing meteor from another dream and were now not just dead and hungry but also radioactive and able to shoot death rays from their fingertips.

Unfortunately, all the zombies in tonight's episode looked like Mrs. Everwiner, and all she had to throw at them were cash registers.

The last thing she dreamed before the scratching noise woke her up was the shadow of a Mrs. Everwiner zombie, three times taller than life, writing an angry letter to the newspaper from the cover of a nearby dark alley.

Fernie sat up on the air mattress she'd be using for a bed until the moving company showed up with the family's furniture, noticing that it was still dark outside.

She wouldn't have minded being awake for a while, as long as there was something to do, but her new bedroom, with its blank walls not yet adorned with posters of movie monsters and its floor not yet covered with a litter of toys and its space not yet taken up with shelves stuffed to bursting with scary books, was not yet a promising place to spend time when everybody else in the house was sleeping.

Then the scratching noise began again, followed by an angry hiss.

She flipped on the flashlight that was her only lamp for now and used it to follow the commotion to the corner next to her clothes closet, where a small but important battle was being fought atop a pyramid of cardboard boxes she hadn't unpacked yet.

"Harrington," she said.

That could have explained everything. Harrington was a typical cat in that most of the things he did only made sense coming from a cat. A cat will spend an hour licking a spot on the floor that tastes just like every other spot on the floor. Or he'll pick a desperate fight with a shower curtain that won't end until it surrenders. Or he'll crawl into a tight, cramped space and wail until someone notices him, then leave as if he doesn't know that he was acting trapped just thirty seconds before. These are all things that seem perfectly sensible to cats.

Harrington seemed to be very angry at the wall. His tail bristling at three times its normal size, his eyes as round as dinner plates, he stared down what looked like a perfectly featureless expanse of wall and slashed at it, angering the wall not at all.

Fernie asked, "What's the matter, boy?"

Harrington meowed that special kind of cat meow all cat owners know, the one that means "I'm not just a dumb cat imagining things. There's something here!"

Of course, in order to look at Fernie and meow such a complicated meow, Harrington had to turn his attention away from the thing that was upsetting him so much, which meant that it had a chance to pop up from its hiding place between the cardboard places and swat at his tail.

The thing swatting him looked a little like Harrington, but it was also as flat as a piece of paper and as dark as the lenses in Fernie's favorite pair of sunglasses.

It was not unusual for Harrington to pick a fight with his shadow, since Harrington was a cat and fighting his own shadow was part of the job he signed up for the very day he was born. But this was the first time Fernie had ever seen Harrington's shadow do something Harrington himself hadn't done.

Harrington yowled and became a ball of enraged fur leaping five feet straight up.

The shadow Harrington jumped straight up, too. Its shadow paw whacked Harrington's real butt three times in a row before Harrington spun around in midair to fight back.

The two landed in an angry ball of cat, real fur and shadow fur exploding in tufts.

Then the shadow Harrington raced out of Fernie's bedroom, and Harrington gave chase.

Fernie had just woken up from a sound sleep and wasn't thinking as fast as she would have in the middle of the day, so it took her a few seconds to remember everything that had happened with Snooks and what she'd been told by Gustav Gloom.

She hadn't shared any of the strange conversation with her sister or father; in Pearlie's case because she wanted to keep the wonderful strangeness of their new neighborhood to herself for a while yet, and in her father's case because the last thing she wanted was for the safety-minded Mr. What to find out he'd moved his daughters into a place where shadows got up and walked around by themselves. Her father would have immediately piled the whole family into the car to head back to some other neighborhood without haunted houses.

Life would be *boring* again.

But all of that could still happen if Harrington and the shadow Harrington woke everybody.

Fernie swung her legs off the air mattress and slipped her feet into the slippers she'd made her father buy, the ones that looked like little Frankenstein's monster heads. They didn't quite match the little werewolf heads that covered her pajamas, but it was the middle of the night, so she didn't think she'd run into anybody who'd complain about the inconsistency.

Gripping her flashlight, she headed into the hallway. The house was dark, and neither cat nor cat shadow seemed to be making noise anymore, but she wanted to make sure that everything was okay. So she moved on toward the kitchen, first peeking her head into the bedroom next to hers, which belonged to Pearlie. Pearlie's eyes were shut and her mouth was wide open. As Fernie watched, she paused midsnore to close her mouth and swallow.

Fernie moved farther down the hallway and passed her father's bedroom, where he was snoring, too, the manual of office safety procedures he'd been reading before bed lying facedown across his chest. As always, he slept with one hand resting protectively on his first-aid kit in case an emergency arose and he needed it during the night.

It occurred to her that this was not the first time that he looked lonely—he had since her mother had left on her latest expedition.

Either way, it didn't look to Fernie like her father or her sister were going to be waking up anytime soon, which was a good thing. She could straighten out this whole business without bothering either of them. She padded away down the hall and entered the combination living room and dining room next to their new kitchen.

Harrington stood on the shelf by the picture

window, his back arched, his tail puffy, a low growl rumbling at the back of his throat.

Fernie didn't know why Harrington was so frozen with fear until she followed his gaze to the light from the window all the way to the opposite wall where it covered a space almost big enough to qualify as a movie screen. The image on that wall was the shadow Harrington as big as a full-grown tiger. Its breath felt hot on Fernie's skin, and when it swiped at her for daring to look it in the eyes, she felt the wind of something heavy and clawed cutting the air in front of her face.

The shadow Harrington tensed and pounced.

Fernie wrapped her arms around her head and ducked, just as the dark and imposing shape seemed to fill the room. She felt a slash on her right arm and almost cried out before the shadow cat thumped against the floor behind her.

As she turned, she saw the three claw marks on her right wrist, just behind the rip the shadow cat had torn in her pajama sleeve.

She spun and saw Harrington become a black-and-white blur as he fled toward the kitchen, the shape of the much larger and much more dangerous shadow Harrington in close pursuit behind him.

She was watching as Harrington leaped up to the sill of the kitchen window and as the looming form of the shadow Harrington, no longer quite as big as it had been but still wild and angry and more than a match for a cat who for all his life had only needed to meow to get fed twice a day, leaped at him.

Earlier tonight, Mr. What had made a point of leaving the inner glass pane up a crack, saying that fresh air cleans all the germs out of an empty house, and it's not good to leave a new house crawling with all the germs from whoever lived there last.

The safety precaution allowed Harrington to rip a hole in the screen in order to get away from the shadowy monster cat. He yowled and shoved his head against the mesh, widening a small tear that had been there already, and was half in and half out of the window in a heartbeat, his hind legs and pudgy rear end wriggling as he forced himself through the opening.

Fernie yelled, "No, Harrington! Stop!"

She leaped to the window just in time to see Harrington cross the white circle of light under the nearest streetlight, a black-and-white bullet that should have cast a shadow but somehow did not. The shadow Harrington also raced across that same light, a patch of darkness in the shape of a cat that should have had a cat but somehow did not.

The cat that cast no shadow and the shadow that cast no cat both slipped in between the bars of the fence that surrounded the Gloom house and disappeared into the shifting patches of deeper darkness.

"No!" Fernie cried.

There was no time to wake up her father or even Pearlie for help. The whole story would have gotten bogged down in the part about the giant vicious monster shadow cat. Fernie might have made them believe her after a dozen or more tries, but all that time Harrington would be lost, out of his mind with panic and getting further into whatever trouble awaited him.

So she just gripped her flashlight tighter, opened the front door, and ran outside in her werewolf-head pajamas and Frankenstein's-monster slippers.

She stopped only once at the curb to look left and right and (because her father would have wanted it) up before crossing the street . . .

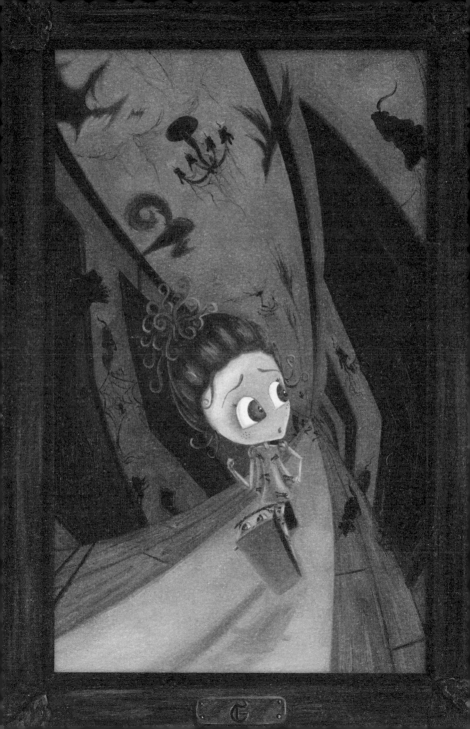

CHAPTER FIVE
"THE PEOPLE TAKER IS LOOSE"

Fernie What stood at the iron fence and shone her flashlight into the darkness. It didn't help much.

She waved the beam around. "Come on, Harrington! Want some noogums?"

Noogums, the family term for the smelly, brown canned glop that constituted most of Harrington's diet, was one of the human phrases he definitely understood, along with *good cat*, *bedtime*, and—thanks to Fernie's dad—*emergency safety procedures*.

Normally, a cry of *noogums* brought Harrington running. But the only cat answer from within the shifting darkness of the Gloom property was a distant wail followed by an angry hiss.

"Harrington! You come back here right *now*!"

As anybody who owns a cat could have predicted, that didn't work even a little bit.

Fernie swung the flashlight beam across the Gloom yard, finding nothing between the fence and the house but the smoky blackness that Gustav seemed to have instead of a lawn. It was only when the light passed the Gloom family's front door that she spotted a familiar shape cowering on the front steps just before the two giant front doors. It was Harrington, whose eyes glowed green the way cats' eyes do when light hits them just right. The second he saw that he was being looked at, he let out the most pitiful of all possible meows, which was very pitiful indeed.

Though he sat in the center of the spotlight, he cast no shadow.

Fernie called to him again, shouting, "Noogums!" in a way that promised the biggest bowl of noogums any cat had ever seen.

Harrington looked interested, but cats prefer claims like that to be verified.

"Stupid cat," Fernie muttered.

This was not a very nice thing to say, but it happened to be true.

Fernie's arm had started to hurt where the shadow Harrington had clawed her, so she wasn't exactly eager to face that strange beast again. But the only other choices were to go back home with her cat still in danger or to stay at the fence promising him noogums all night long, so she inched along the row of iron bars until she reached the gate, which was unlocked and swung inward with a push. The little tendrils of fog curled at the edges of the Gloom property, melting almost at once wherever they spread past the fence line.

"This is your last chance, stupid cat! You can come out by yourself and have some noogums, or you can wait there for me to get you and be in *big* trouble!"

Harrington licked his paw and considered his options. Any fear he might have had of the giant shadow cat, wherever it was, seemed to have evaporated out of his little head.

Fernie stepped over the property line onto the Gloom estate. To her it felt like brushing aside a soft silk curtain and walking into a room where the air was cooler and the light was dimmer and the floor was the source of a draft.

Between the gate and the steps to those big doors where Harrington sat licking his paw, she heard a number of soft voices murmuring things she couldn't understand. Somebody said, "Ooh, pretty." Somebody else said, "Another one for the People Taker." A third voice said, "Poor girl," in a voice as sad as the one Fernie's aunt Sybil fell into whenever she watched sad movies where the family dog dies at the end.

Fernie didn't want to think much about who those voices belonged to and what they were saying, but they didn't bother her even half as much as the sudden squeal of rusty hinges.

Those big front doors were opening.

"Oh no!" Fernie cried as she started to run.

She knew that Harrington, like all cats, loved open doors.

Cats love open doors even if they have no idea what's on the other side.

In fact, cats love open doors *especially* when they don't know what's on the other side.

She didn't have time to realize that this was also a pretty good description of the mistake she was making by passing through the front gate of the Gloom estate without telling anybody where she was going . . . and by racing up those three front steps after her cat.

By the time she reached the front stoop, Harrington's question mark of an upright tail was wagging a little good-bye wave as he nosed his way into the darkness.

"No!" Fernie yelled. "Harrington, stop!"

She grabbed for him, but by then she was past the front door herself, watching the tip of his tail turn the corner at the end of the long front hall.

The end of the hall was too far away to make sense even for a house this big, and the blackness too thick even for a house this dark.

When Fernie shone her flashlight down the hall, the beam had no trouble casting light on the framed paintings lining the walls or the dusty chandeliers hanging from the ceiling or the long, narrow dingy red carpet marking the path she'd have to walk if she decided to go any farther. But it wouldn't light up that blackness at the end of the hall.

Fernie almost turned back. As much as she hated to give up on Harrington, she had read a number of books and been to a number of movies about haunted houses and knew that the people reading those books or watching those movies always yell at the girl who walks deeper into the haunted house for being so stupid.

Fernie had to admit that this was pretty much the same situation, and if her life ever became a book or a movie, she wouldn't want anybody reading it to call her stupid for continuing to chase her cat into darkness. So she glanced over her shoulder just long enough to make sure that the way out was still clear and saw that it wasn't.

The doorway was full of dark shapes coming in after her.

There were too many to count: things shaped like people and things shaped like dogs and things shaped like big black birds and things shaped like giant clutching hands and things that looked like about six or seven of all those other things mashed together so they didn't look like people or dogs or birds or hands but what happens when you melt them all together into a big wriggling mess.

The Harrington shadow was just one of them, and though it wasn't as big as a tiger anymore, it was still a cat Fernie could see through. It leaped past all the other shadows to dart through the gap between Fernie's legs and down the hall after the real cat.

The dark shapes approaching her all spoke in soft, whispery voices.

"Little girl," one said.

"You're trespassing," another said.

"You shouldn't be out tonight," a third said.

"The People Taker is loose," a fourth warned.

They reached for her, their long, gray see-through hands giving off a smoky mist wherever they passed through the bright light of Fernie's flashlight beam.

Fernie did something she had never done before in her life, something that she had often promised herself she would never ever do if attacked by monsters. She screamed like a girl.

She turned around and ran farther into the house, her Frankenstein's monster—head slippers pounding the red carpet as she fled down the long hallway. She ran past framed paintings that didn't seem to be anything but big black squares, past walls that seemed to shift and dance as she ran by, past decorative vases twice her size and dark shapes that poked their gray heads out of them as if disturbed from their slumber. Other dark shapes raced along the walls and ceiling, their long arms reaching out for her as she ran, and their voices whispering things like "Get out," and "You should not be here," and "Stay away from the Pit."

Scared as she was, Fernie didn't like that "Stay away from the Pit" business, especially since she still couldn't see past the darkness at the end of the hall. It crossed her mind that maybe she should stop, but somehow that idea didn't get to her legs, which were quite happy running.

She ran past the end of the hall into a grand parlor of some kind, many stories taller than the house had looked from across the street. There were at least a dozen ornate staircases, each leading to balconies on upper floors, each crowded with more shadowy figures peering over the railing and pointing at Fernie. She could not see a ceiling, just an endless field of darkness as vast as the sky. But the walls were alive with shadows, including more giant cats and a few giant dogs and a big swarm of something that could only be bats.

The floor was a polished tile of some kind, and when she tried to evade a crowd of looming shapes directly in her path, she went into an uncontrolled slide. Fernie tried to brake before she slid right into them but was moving too fast. Passing through them was like passing through a cold breeze. She grabbed the armrest of a couch to stop herself, fell to her knees, and screeched as others lunged for her again.

"Little girl . . ."

"The People Taker will get you, little girl . . ."

She got up and fled without any particular direction in mind, fleeing down one of a number of hallways branching out from this main room.

More shadows, a mob of them, loomed ahead. Another hallway opened up to her left. She ducked down that one and then another opened to her right, and she was so panicked that she took that one, too, even though she knew by then that these were too many confusing turns and that she was getting herself lost.

Making it all worse somehow was the distant sound of Harrington's meow, somehow just ahead of her and a million miles away at the same time.

The small problem was that she would never find him, not in all of this.

The bigger problem was that she was beginning to doubt that she would ever find her way back to the front door, either.

She started to slow down, at least enough for the doors on both sides of the current hall to stop going by in such a blur. She saw that they didn't match one another. There were bright white doors and dark wooden doors and doors with curved tops and doors too small for mice to get through. There were even a few doorways without actual doors in them, just black openings as hard to see past as the blackness at the end of the entrance hall had been.

By the time she slowed to a stop at a place where two long corridors crossed, she seemed to have traveled miles. Harrington's meow sounded so close that she might have been able to reach out and touch him. But he was nowhere to be seen.

"Cat," she said to him, not knowing if he could hear her but hoping he could, "you and I are going to have a real long talk."

Wherever he was, he meowed, which meant either "I know, I know, this is all my fault," or "It wasn't my idea to move into this neighborhood."

She spun a little because she was dizzy, and she fell down, feeling even more stupid than she'd felt a second before, because after that spin she was no longer quite sure which of the four long hallways around her she'd just come running from. There seemed to be thousands of doors stretching in every direction as far as her eyes could see, but there didn't seem to be any of those dark moving shapes around right now.

She was lost, and she didn't have the slightest idea what to do next. This was not nearly as simple and fun as a mere rickety staircase with loose boards and protruding nails.

She was alarmed to feel her eyes burn in the special way that announces the arrival of tears.

"No," she told herself. "Absolutely not. That will not be helpful at all. You can cry like a baby for an hour, and when you're done, you will still be in the same stupid place with the same stupid problems. Find the stupid cat, then find the stupid way out, and then bawl all you want. But crying now is stupid."

She dabbed at her eyes and turned around in a complete circle, taking another careful look at the four dark corridors stretching away from her. No direction seemed any better than any other. But then she thought of something that made her feel a whole lot better.

When you're lost in a big, confusing place, it helps to have more than one good thing to look for.

Finding Harrington would be a good thing.

Finding the way back out afterward would be even better.

But in the meantime, she'd have a lot of help finding *both* if she could just find that boy, Gustav Gloom.

CHAPTER SIX
THE BEAST IN THE LIBRARY

Fernie started trying the doors and calling Gustav's name along with Harrington's. She didn't find the boy or the cat, but she did find more confusing things.

One door opened up into a room that seemed to be filled with dark shapes that resembled giant rabbits. Another had straight-backed wooden chairs that were running around in circles while making race car noises.

Then she turned a crystal doorknob and found a room so strange that for a few seconds she forgot all the others.

It was the largest library she had ever seen, occupying a circular room with walls that towered all the way from the carpeted floor at the entrance to what looked like miles above her. She craned her neck to follow the shelves as they reached toward the sky and got a headache when she spotted the place far above where all those endless shelves came together at a single dot.

A long ramp of a walkway started at the door and spiraled up along the wall, circling and circling until it also hurt her eyes to see how far up it went. Thin black candles burned along the wooden railing, one every few steps for as far as her eyes could see. Fernie couldn't imagine an army of people with a world of matches ever having the time to light them all, let alone clean up all the wax drippings. They were the only lights around, but there were so many of them—millions, she supposed. They came together high above her head in a flickering light like a sun.

The books all had black leather covers without any visible titles. She ran her pointer finger along a couple of them and, despite not having the time to read any books right now, couldn't resist pulling one off the shelf, just to see what kind of book it was.

It turned out to be the biggest and heaviest book she'd ever held. She struggled with it, placing it flat on the stone floor so she could turn the first page and then the second and then the third.

The pages were all, like so much in that house, as black as night.

She took a closer look at one of the pages and saw from the dim impression of glossy black lettering against glossy black paper that the book wasn't blank, but had words in it the same black color as the paper that could be seen only if you squinted and strained and held the pages at just the right angle, revealing the places where the shiny ink caught just enough of the light to be seen.

Doing everything she could to read just one of those words, a *the*, was so much trouble that she couldn't imagine why anybody would read further to find out "the" what.

She was still straining to return the volume to the shelf where she'd found it when the nearest candles seemed to flicker with a sudden draft and a cold voice high above her explained, "It's an idea."

"What?"

"The book," the voice explained. "It's an idea. Do you know how many great ideas are never born?"

She looked up and thought she could see a man coming down the ramp, maybe a hundred feet above her. "I don't know. A lot?"

The man continued to descend, leaning over the balcony and peering down at her as he went. Fernie couldn't see his face because he had long, stringy hair that hung over his cheeks like a pair of curtains, shading his face from the light of all those flickering candles. His top hat was tall and narrow and bent in the middle.

"More than fffffive?" he said, rolling the *f*.

"I suppose a lot more than five," Fernie guessed.

"More than a hunnnnndred?" he whispered, drawing out the word.

As he descended the long spiral walkway, slowly making his way down to her, Fernie had to keep turning in circles to keep him in sight. "I guess there must be zillions."

"Even more than zzzzzillions," he said, running his black-gloved hand along the railing as he made his way toward her. "A zzzzzillion zzzzzillion zzzzzillion." He made the words sound like the buzzing of wasps.

He was not a shadow. He was a man, though a man who dressed all in black and seemed as much at home in this near darkness as any shadow possibly could. Fernie didn't need to wait until this man reached her to already know that he had nothing good in mind. But there was something about his voice, something about the calm way he spoke and the unhurried way he moved, that kept her rooted in place, unable to make it to the door and run away.

He said, "You have fffffound a library of all the ideas that never came to be; all the great books never written, all the dangeroussssss visions never imagined, all the great inventions that poor men could have built and made themselves rich. Why, that very book you just looked at has what would have been the greatest poem ever written, until some sssssilly man knocked on the poet's door, interrupted his day, took up his time, and put all those great lines right out of his brilliant head and back into the world of shadowsssss. Can you imagine that, Fffffernie? Can you even guesssss what elssssse is hidden here?"

The man in black wasn't the only thing making its way down from high above. Something else clung to the shelves, so high above her that she couldn't make out its exact shape. But it seemed to change its form every time it swung down to the next set of shelves. It reminded her of something. A feeling she knew well, had seen many times, and didn't like.

As she watched, it jumped from one curve of the walkway, many floors up, across the open space to another curve several levels below, clinging to the railing for a second before yet another leap across open space.

It had more arms and legs than Fernie wanted to think about.

Either way, it looked like there was a race over whether the man in black or the monster with the familiar shape was going to get to her first.

"Fffffernie?" asked the man in black, making the first letter of her name sound just like all the air going out of a dying balloon. "I sssssaid, can you guesssss what *else* is hidden in this library?"

He was now only five or six turns of the walkway above her, close enough for her to see that his black suit included the hint of a cape, ending halfway down his back. His pointed, white teeth were like headlights in the blackness that, for the moment, hid the rest of his face.

Fernie found her voice. "How do you know my name?"

"I know a lot of things, Fffffernie. I was watching and listening from a window when you moved in across the street. I found that nice and convenient, because you're exactly the kind of person I like to *take*. But you haven't answered my question. Do you know what elssssse is hidden here?"

"Why don't you just tell me?"

"All the life-saving ideas. All the brilliant strokes of geniusssss that could have saved any number of poor people who found themselves in terrible danger. All the ways they could have gotten off sssssinking ships. All the ways they could have gotten out of burning houses. All the ways they could have essssscaped the bad men like me who were going to *take* them. There are many books here that could help you get away, Fffffernie. Many." The man in black chuckled. "Would you like to know where on the shhhhhelves you'd find them?"

The shapeless monster jumped again, falling past many levels of walkway before wrapping its claws around the railing on the loop of walkway just over the man's head. As she watched, it turned its head, located Fernie, and tensed up, less than a second from jumping down the rest of the way.

Too late, Fernie's legs unfroze. She spun in place and darted for the library door, knowing even as she reached for the crystal doorknob that she was not nearly fast enough, that the monster had already leaped and would land between her and the door.

He landed right in front of her with a powerful *thud*, a wall of fur and muscle and too many arms and legs to count, all between her and the hallway where all she'd had to worry about was being lost.

It should have been close enough to see now, but Fernie's eyes refused to make sense of any one part of it, from the mouth that seemed to be as big as the rest of it put together, to the eyes that looked like eyes only until she looked at them, and then looked like other mouths. Its two biggest arms, that were so much bigger than Fernie herself, still looked ridiculously small compared to the rest of it. None of it made sense.

Fernie couldn't have described it with a thousand words or painted a decent picture of it with a warehouse of watercolors, the help of the best artist in the world, and a white wall the size of a barn. But as the thing reached for her, taking its time, she suddenly knew where she had seen it before.

At night sometimes, when she'd been so tired or lazy that she forgot to throw her dirty clothes in the hamper and instead just tossed them onto the back of her desk chair . . . sometimes she woke up and the light coming in through the crack of the door shone on the combination of clothes and chair and made a shapeless but terrible monster.

Without thinking, she did what she'd always done to make it go away.

She shone her flashlight at it.

The result was almost as terrible as letting the thing get her. The circle of light at the end of the beam lit up a part of its face that looked like a bath mat somebody had tossed into a mud puddle. There were more eyes and shapes that looked like angry black worms. But the touch of the flashlight beam made the monster cry out and fall back, smoke rising from fresh burns on its skin. It slammed against the door, still between Fernie and escape as it reached for her with arms like tree trunks. Fernie ducked and felt an awful hot wind pass through the air right over her head.

"Very nice," said the man in black. "That's one fffffine idea that won't gather dust on these shelves. But it's only a *sssssmall* idea, one that won't save you for more than a few sssssseconds. I'll still get to *take* you."

There was something about the way he kept saying *take* that made the word the most terrible thing Fernie had ever heard.

Using both hands to hold her flashlight before her, Fernie could think of nothing to do but keep it pointed at the monster's face.

Then it charged her again.

Fernie was sure she was dead, but it blundered right past her and slammed into the shelves with a mighty crash. Books flew everywhere. The impossible monster reached one impossible arm around its impossible back to swipe at its impossible shoulders.

It was only when it staggered back into the center of the floor and toward her again that Fernie was able to tear her gaze away from the awful mess it had instead of a proper face long enough to pay attention to the form riding those shoulders: the strangely familiar dark outline of a young girl, punching it again and again with fists Fernie could see through.

The beast swiped at this girl shape but couldn't seem to reach her no matter how hard it tried.

High above her, the man in black said, "Oh, well. I can always come down there and *take* you myself."

Then somebody grabbed Fernie by her left wrist and yanked, hard. She found herself being pulled toward the shelves with all their unreadable books, caught a glimpse of a pale hand pulling her along, and found herself kneeling in a narrow, cramped little closet just as a panel slid down and locked everything in the library out.

One tremendous crash later, the panel cracked, but held.

Fernie shone her flashlight at the face of the boy who had pulled her into the closet.

"Hello," said Gustav Gloom.

CHAPTER SEVEN
WATCHING OUT FOR THE DINOSAUR POOP

Despite its being the middle of the night, Gustav still wore a little black suit with a little black tie. Either he dressed up all the time because he had important business meetings all day, or it was the only thing in his closet and he had to use it for everything.

Fernie knew that she should have been grateful for being rescued, but the past hour had left her so irritated that she had to spill some anger out in order to make room for actual thinking. So she put both hands on Gustav's chest, shoved him angrily back against the wall of the closet with a *thump*, and yelled, "Those are the kinds of things you have slinking around your *house*?"

Gustav Gloom wore no expression on his pale little face. "Yes."

"Your *house*? Really?"

"Yes."

"Are they your family?"

"Oh no," he said. "I wouldn't want to have them for family. They're more like unwanted visitors."

"Why don't you just throw them out then?"

"There's no point. They'd just come back."

"Who are they?"

"I thought they told you. That's the People Taker and his pet, the Beast."

"So what on earth are you doing with a *People Taker* and a *Beast* in your *house*?"

Gustav Gloom said, "Hiding, mostly."

Fernie felt her jaw fall open as if it had been held shut only by a little string and that string had now broken.

"Or running away," Gustav said. "That works, too." He frowned. "You know, I never actually had any long conversations with him, but based on the way it worked out for you, it's not something I'm eager to try. Why did you?"

"Because I didn't know what he was!" Fernie yelled. "We don't have People Takers where I come from!"

"Of course you do. Where else do you think he started *taking* people from in the first place?"

Fernie managed a very quiet, "What?"

"Out there," Gustav said, "in the world where you live, he was just a very bad man. He did bad things to people because he liked to. He called it *taking* them. I don't know how many he *took* that way, but it was an awful lot."

"What did he do with them?"

"Nothing they appreciated."

"Didn't they complain?"

"After a while, they couldn't."

Gustav seemed to be trying so hard to spare her the terrible details that Fernie decided she didn't need to hear them. "Didn't anybody try to stop him?"

"Oh, sure, lots of people. From what I understand, he only hopped our fence in the first place because the police and the FBI and a bunch of angry families were closing in and he needed a hiding place. But that was about the worst thing that could have happened, because after a few days of running around in here looking for a way out, he entered the wrong room and fell into the Pit, all the way down to the Dark Country where Lord Obsidian found him and put him back to work doing what he was good at."

This new name, Lord Obsidian, sounded

even worse than the People Taker, but Fernie was not quite ready to explore that yet. "*Taking* people."

"Uh-huh," Gustav said.

"So he's been doing this while he's been hiding in your house."

"That's right. He goes out at night and goes looking for people to *take*. It's his job, kind of."

Fernie remembered all the mysterious disappearances Mrs. Everwiner had mentioned. "Then why haven't *you* done anything to stop him? Why haven't you called the police?"

"We don't have a phone."

"Why didn't you just warn people? Or ask somebody in the neighborhood for help?"

Gustav stopped between one step and the next, wearing an expression that could not have been any worse if he'd been hit in the face by a board. "It's not that easy. People on the other side of the fence—especially grown-ups—don't always want to talk to me."

"I talked to you."

"There aren't many like you."

"Okay, so if it was just you," Fernie asked, "why haven't you snuck up behind him and pushed him over a balcony or something?"

"It's not that easy," Gustav said. "He has

the Beast helping him. I haven't even been able to get close."

"Sounds like a lame excuse to me when there are innocent people being *taken*."

Gustav remained silent.

"And another thing," she asked. "What does this Lord Obsidian, whoever he is, do with the people this People Taker . . . *takes*?"

Gustav hesitated, then he heaved a sigh of tremendous sadness that struck Fernie as the very first sound he'd made that matched the gray, unsmiling expression on his face.

"You don't want to know."

Fernie almost protested, but realized that it happened to be true, at least for the moment. Her head was already so crowded with thoughts of People Takers and Beasts and houses bigger on the inside than they were on the outside that she was not yet ready to absorb any more terrifying information.

Then Gustav said, "Come on. I'll take you someplace a little safer."

She was so grateful to him for saying something that made some kind of sense that she put all her other questions away in a box for later. "Okay."

He squeezed past her, did something unseen

to the panel, and opened it back up again.

Fernie feared that the library would be on the other side and that the People Taker and his pet would still be there, waiting to do whatever awful things he had meant by *taking* her.

But this time the opening led to a flight of stone stairs, shiny with water dripping down from a low ceiling, which curved up a narrow passage lit by torches. The torches didn't seem to be having much trouble staying lit even though the water coming down from above was so heavy that it was just a couple of clouds and a flash of lightning away from becoming a thunderstorm. Loud smashing, banging, crashing, and roaring noises, together a lot like how Fernie imagined a prehistoric jungle would sound, echoed from up above.

Gustav began climbing the stairs. "It shouldn't be too bad up this way. He's only a *People* Taker, so he never bothers the dinosaurs."

Fernie had been about to follow him, but now she stopped in midstep. "Dinosaurs."

Four steps above her, Gustav said, "Well, yes. We're headed for their bedroom."

"Your house has a bedroom for *dinosaurs*?"

"Of course it does. Where else would they sleep?"

Fernie rubbed the spot at the bridge of her nose that her father sometimes rubbed. She had noticed that this habit of his seemed to help him understand things a little better, but it didn't help her one bit. Apparently, she didn't have any brains in her nose.

She wasn't doing herself much good here at the bottom of what looked like dungeon stairs, so she put one foot in front of the other and pretty soon she was following Gustav, at least in the sense of walking behind him, if not in the sense of understanding any of this.

Gustav chatted away. "They're not really dinosaurs, anyway. They're dinosaur shadows."

He had disappeared around the next bend of the stairs before he seemed to notice that she'd stopped climbing again. His pale little head popped around the curve of the wall to peer at her. "What?"

Fernie spoke very slowly as if afraid that the words would jam together if she didn't let them out one at a time. "Shadow dinosaurs . . . like shadow cats."

"Well, not exactly like shadow cats. They're much larger."

Fernie grew irritated with him for changing

the subject. "I came across the street looking for my cat, Harrington."

He came down a step. "Why would you think your cat was over here?"

"I saw his *shadow* chase him here."

"Oh," he said. "That makes sense."

"How does that make sense?"

"It just does," Gustav Gloom said. "Cats are always starting fights with their shadows. They're much better at seeing their shadows move than people are. I'd better help you find him."

This was, of course, exactly what Fernie had wanted in the first place, but right now it was only as useful as a hamburger stand on the ground to a hungry girl riding the roller coaster: a good place to wind up eventually, but not at all helpful when she still had to ride wherever the tracks took her.

Getting more of the big picture with every sentence, she said, "I ran away from some other shadows in the front hall and saw a few hundred others in that other big room up front. Another one, a girl's shadow, attacked the Beast for me, just like that."

"There are a lot of shadows here," Gustav said. "Most of them don't talk to me much, but sometimes they do me favors. Maybe one took a liking to you."

"*Shadows* live here."

"It's not so unusual," he said. "They live in your house, too."

"But you're *not* a shadow."

"Do I *look* like a shadow?"

"No," Fernie said. "You just look like a kid who never gets any sun."

"That's what I am, more or less."

"So how did you end up being raised in a shadow house?"

Gustav shrugged. "I was adopted."

The invisible string holding Fernie's jaw shut seemed to snap again. She closed her mouth with more difficulty than that act had ever given her and continued to follow the strange, pale boy up the next four turns of the spiral staircase until they reached the top, the bedroom of the shadow dinosaurs.

It wasn't anything at all like what Fernie had imagined. Somehow she'd pictured a typical boy's bedroom ten stories tall, with furniture to fit, including bunk beds eight stories tall, a gigantic wicker toy chest, and bright blue wallpaper with rocket ships on it. She'd even imagined a tyrannosaurus rex in a striped red T-shirt and khaki shorts sitting at a gigantic desk playing video games. She hadn't really expected any of this because it would have been ridiculous, but it was the image that had come to mind, and it wasn't all that unreasonable given how much very real ridiculousness the Gloom house had.

Instead, what she saw when the top of the staircase opened up into a much larger room was a dark gray mist over what felt like, but didn't even come close to looking like, a dense tropical jungle. The air smelled like the elephant house at every zoo she'd ever been to, which as far as Fernie was concerned answered a question she'd never before this day had any reason to ask: whether shadow dinosaurs made shadow dinosaur poop. Fernie wasn't sure that she wanted to venture into that murk, where the only warning she would have of any nearby hungry mouths would be when she suddenly found herself inside one. "Can we take a break here until I get used to this?"

"How long will that take?" Gustav asked.

"How about just until I get used to knowing that I'll never get used to it?"

"Okay," Gustav said agreeably. "But when I say we have to hurry up and go, we have to hurry up and go. Otherwise the dinosaurs may be a problem."

After a moment, Fernie sat. "How many of them are out there?"

He said, "All of them."

Had she possessed a dinosaur throat of her own right now, her own growl would have been the most ill-tempered in the room. "But how many *is* that? Four? Five? A hundred?"

Gustav shrugged. "I don't know exactly. However many real dinosaurs there ever were, that's how many shadow dinosaurs we have."

"There must have been millions of dinosaurs. How can they all fit in one dinosaur bedroom?"

"Shadows don't really take up space," Gustav said. "They can walk through one another and over one another and be in the same place at the same time. Overcrowding isn't something that bothers them."

Fernie said, "But the dinosaurs died a long time ago. Why would there still be shadow dinosaurs?"

"They're *shadows*," he said a little peevishly as if he was beginning to get tired of repeating this simple point. "They don't really live or die, and they don't go away just because the things they shadowed went away. They're around as long as they want to be."

Fernie said, "Then the same thing would be true of all the shadows of all the people who ever lived. They would still be running around somewhere, even if the people they shadowed died long ago."

"Right," Gustav said.

"Tell me again why you think this is safer than the library."

"The library's not all that bad. I get books from there all the time. It was only bad today for a while because the People Taker took his Beast hunting for you there. I bet you if we go back later it'll be just fine."

"But you took me from a room with one beast in it to a room with I don't know how many shadow dinosaurs in it. How's that *safe*?"

"I didn't say it was *safe*," Gustav Gloom said. "I said it was saf*er*."

Fernie thought back and, yes, that was exactly what he had said. It was safer, she supposed, in much the same way that a kid throwing a rock at you is better than a bigger kid throwing a bigger rock at you.

She heard a tremendous crash, and a flock

of shadow birds scattered, cawing just to make their own opinion known. "What kind of house is this?"

"A shadow house," Gustav Gloom said as if explaining something obvious. "One of only about ten houses like it in the whole world. I don't know where all the other houses are, but I heard once that they have one in Liechtenstein."

Fernie, who couldn't remember ever hearing of any country named Liechtenstein, wondered if it was a real place or an imaginary one. "And?"

"Like the other houses, it's got all the bits and pieces of every house that people ever thought about building but didn't. That's why it's so big inside—it's like a world all by itself. It makes a perfect place for shadows to go whenever they want some free time away from the things they shadow. We also have a pit leading back to the Dark Country where shadows come from, but most of my family avoids that; there's a big civil war going on down there, so this world's a whole lot nicer."

Fernie, who was still coming up with questions faster than she was getting answers, started to say something else, but Gustav cocked his head and put out a little pale hand to shut her up.

He listened some more as if picking one small sound out of the many wild and savage noises spilling from the gray fog of the dinosaur bedroom. Then he shouted, "I see a way through! Follow me!"

Before she could ask why and where, he had darted into the shadow jungle.

The immediate reaction to this from the inhabitants of the dinosaur bedroom was a sudden explosion of roars and growls and snarls, complete with the crash of trees and the thud of massive pounding feet.

Without quite realizing it, Fernie added a gasp and scream to that collection of noises. She jumped to her feet, torn between the sensible need to run away as fast as she could and the awareness that she didn't have a ghost of an idea which direction that would be.

Then Gustav called out to her, from what seemed like a tremendous distance away. *"Fernie . . . !"*

A long time ago, Fernie had heard courage described to her as temporarily forgetting to be afraid. So, deciding to forget her fear, she ran out into the shadow jungle herself.

Of course, she remembered her fear again

after she'd pounded ten steps and left the entrance to the stairs somewhere in the gray clouds behind her. It was not a nice thing to suddenly remember. Nobody ever enjoys being reminded that they're running blind into a foggy room filled with the shadows of prehistoric beasts. Or at least nobody ever *would* enjoy it, if things like that happened to people more often.

But she was well inside the room and running as fast as she could and stopping would have been even more crazy than entering it in the first place. So she gritted her teeth and ran faster, her Frankenstein's monster—head slippers pounding against a soft surface that felt like rich forest soil but that was actually *upstairs in somebody's house.*

"Fernie!" Gustav yelled, somewhere ahead of her. "This way!"

Following his voice, she veered to her right, feeling shadow ferns brush against her face. The ground all around her shook as something she couldn't see charged at her from behind. She shrieked, dodged a looming shape ahead, almost tripped over what felt like a tree root, and pumped her arms harder as she forced herself to speed up even more. She found herself breaking out of the jungle and entering something that felt like tall grass, running faster than she ever had.

"This way!" Gustav cried.

He was not so far away now. Fernie could see his serious little shape through the fog. She was so relieved, even though she couldn't imagine that they were out of danger yet.

She ran, his voice leading her through more shifting patches of darkness and light to his side. The dinosaur cacophony continued, but they seemed to have been left far behind, and Gustav had stopped. He wasn't even breathing hard.

"See?"

She punched him in the upper arm. He said the same thing most people who get punched say.

"Ow!"

"Serves you right," Fernie growled.

"What did I do?"

"You left me back there."

"So? I knew you would follow me."

"Through a room filled with shadow dinosaurs!"

"Apparently so."

Every time this boy answered a question, he left Fernie with two more. About twenty of them vied to be the next one out of her mouth.

"How can you stand this place?"

"It's not so bad," Gustav said. "Don't you have dangerous things on your side of the street? Earthquakes? Wars? Blizzards? Coral snakes? Loose boards with sharp nails? People who drive their cars up onto sidewalks because they're too busy trying to pick up the spare change that fell near the gas pedal? How can *you* stand it?"

It was the kind of question Fernie's father might have asked. "It's not so bad."

"Exactly!" Gustav cried as if he'd just won the argument. He started walking.

Fernie was left wondering whether the house would kill her before she killed him . . .

CHAPTER EIGHT
PROTECTIVE SAFETY RAILINGS ARE NOT INVOLVED

The door out of the dinosaur bedroom was not up against a wall but standing all by itself in the middle of the gray fog. Fernie walked around it twice just to make sure it was exactly what it seemed to be: a freestanding door.

She said nothing. She'd gotten a lot better during her time in the Gloom mansion at just letting stuff like this pass.

This was fortunate, since making a fuss about the door would have obligated her to make another fuss about the hallway they found on the other side.

For no apparent reason, it was tilted, with the floor and the adjoining walls leaning forty-five degrees to one side. It was impossible to walk on the floor without falling all the way over against the wall, and just as impossible to walk on that wall without falling all the way over onto the floor. The only real place to walk was the narrow edge where the floor and the wall met, where a thick layer of dust had collected.

When you're visiting somebody's house and nothing in it makes any sense to you and you've pretty much done nothing but ask one question after another, you gradually start to figure out that if you don't stop asking questions, you'll never get anywhere at all. So instead, Fernie pointed at the fresh cat prints that had collected in the dust, which emerged from the door to the dinosaur bedroom and trotted off into the distance. "These look fresh. Could those be Harrington's?"

Gustav nodded. "That's the way to the dining room. He must have thought he could beg something to eat there."

That did sound like Harrington, even if it also sounded like almost every other cat who had ever lived. So they set off, Gustav leading the way and Fernie following along.

He turned out to be incredibly agile. He hopped from floor to wall and from wall to floor like a monkey. Keeping up wasn't the easiest thing Fernie had ever done, because she'd never practiced walking in a place like this, and the narrow edge between the floor and the wall wasn't as wide as a human foot wearing a cumbersome Frankenstein's monster–head slipper. The only way Fernie could manage the trick was to walk with one foot on the tilted floor and the other on the tilted wall, trying not to slip.

It was enough to make her think about everything her father would have had to say about the terrible accidents that could befall a person in a house where corridors were built this way. And of course her father would have covered the Gloom house in protective safety railings.

Fernie didn't know how she would go about ridding Gustav's house of its various dangers, but she was pretty sure that protective safety railings wouldn't be involved.

She worried about how her father would feel if something bad did happen to her tonight. He was a good dad most of the time, even if he spent his days dividing the world into places where people could get hurt by walking or sitting or standing still. He didn't deserve to be sad when he was already so busy being frightened. And it would be even worse for Pearlie. If Fernie didn't make it home, Pearlie would turn forty before she was ever allowed to leave the house by herself again.

And then there was Mom to worry about.

Mom was only in the country a couple of months out of the year. She was famous for becoming the first woman to ever attempt to climb Mount Everest all by herself, blindfolded. It was one of the bravest things anybody had ever tried to do, and Fernie's mom had not only done it without an ounce of fear, but survived, making it all the way to the summit and back in record time, during a blizzard, without ever removing the blindfold from her eyes.

But that was Fernie's mom: living a life of endless adventure, laughing in the face of danger. She and Fernie's dad managing not only to meet but also to have anything to talk about was just one of life's little miracles.

Mom would be upset, too. She was a good mom when she was around, even if she wasn't around much. And if Fernie got hurt tonight, she would probably blame herself for being off on some mountaintop. Fernie didn't want that. After all, she hardly needed another parent worrying about keeping her safe when the one she did have worried so much, he made her use protective covers on paper clips.

By the time Fernie began to pay attention to

where they were again, they had been following the paw prints for about ten minutes. Dark shapes, vaguely resembling people but stretched out to many times their natural length, had begun to emerge from the various doors lining the corridor and floated alongside them, chattering away in strange languages Fernie didn't know and some that she wasn't even certain could be called languages at all. A very small number of the shapes spoke in sentences Fernie understood, saying things like "Hi, Gustav," and "Oh, good, you found her" and "*Tsk, tsk*, what's a girl like her doing out this time of night?" and, again, "The People Taker is loose."

Then one particular shape circled Gustav twice, seemed to hug him, and surprised Fernie by fluttering back her way to embrace her as well. "Fernie!" it cried. "I'm so glad that Gustav found you! I heard you'd come for a visit and was so afraid that the People Taker would get you first!"

Its hug felt like a cool wind just before a summer rain. Fernie asked it, "Have we met?"

"Not really. Well, sort of. In a way. It's open to interpretation."

That was helpful. "Who are you?"

"I'm the shadow of a man named Mr. Notes. He visited here once. I'm afraid he wasn't a very nice man, and I was pretty much already fed up with his behavior when we came here a few years ago, so I didn't go with him when he left."

Fernie wasn't sure she liked this information at all. "So the real Mr. Notes doesn't have a shadow anymore?"

"Well," the shadow Mr. Notes said, "it's not like he made following him around all the time a barrel of laughs."

Fernie was still struggling with the concept. "So he doesn't cast a shadow at all now?"

"No, of course not."

"What happens to him when he's out in the sun?"

Gustav Gloom and the runaway shadow of Mr. Notes both answered that one at the same time. "He gets hot."

Even as Fernie wrestled with this, the corridor grew more crowded from the many dark shapes joining the mob. Soon the air was so thick with them that they began to merge together, forming a great gray cloud that no longer looked like it was made up of people, but instead like a thunderhead that had not yet decided to drop its first drop of rain. The shadow of Mr. Notes was whisked away in the crowd, and the others seemed to realize how jammed together they were, because their many different voices started to say things like "Oops" and "Pardon me" and "Hey, stop shoving" and "Excuse me, madam, you have your elbow in my eye." Forcing her way through it began to feel less like walking around inside a house and more like being waist-deep in warm water and trying to get to the other side of the swimming pool.

Then all of a sudden the tilted corridor opened out into a vast dining room, less like a proper room than a wider corridor extending left and right as far as the eye could see. An endless oak banquet table, just as long, sat in the center of the room, its ends invisible in the distance. The shadow shapes of crystal chandeliers hung from the arched ceiling every twenty feet or so, not so much casting light as making places where it was less dark.

A rich feast that seemed to include roast turkey and glazed ham and bowls of spaghetti and cupcakes and hamburgers—all also made of shadow-stuff, unfortunately for Fernie's growling stomach—sat piled on the table, also for an infinite distance in either direction. The hundreds of shadow shapes emerging from the various doors and open hallways on both sides of the room wasted no time claiming the empty seats and attacking the meal with great abandon. Most of them had terrible table manners.

Many of the assembled shadows cried out to greet Gustav as he and Fernie entered. One said, "Hey, kiddo! You're late for dinner!" Another said, "How are you doing? Who's your friend?" A third warned, "You do know the People Taker is loose, right?" A fourth worried, "Do I have a piece of spinach stuck between my front teeth?"

Gustav waved. "Hello, everybody! Anybody seen a cat?"

A dozen of the nearest shadows answered all at once, few of their comments helpful. One said, "You mean, ever? Yeah, I saw one in 1933." Then another, closer to Fernie than all the rest, spoke up in rich, cultured tones that would not have been out of place coming from the mouth of a queen.

"You must be talking about the black-and-white cat that came trotting through here a few minutes ago."

Fernie couldn't help crying out, "Yes! That would be Harrington! Did you see which way he went?"

"Come here, dear. Let me take a look at you."

Fernie couldn't tell which of the shadow diners was speaking, but Gustav took her by the arm and led her over to the appropriate seat.

Up until this moment, all the shadows Fernie had met in Gustav's house were just clouds of darkness in the shapes of whatever cast them. But this close up, beneath the light of the chandeliers, the faces and features of all the diners grew clearer, picking up more and more detail until they looked not much different from how the real people whose shadows they were might have looked in dim light.

The one who'd called them over was a chubby-cheeked, shiny-faced lady with kind eyes, round shoulders, what Fernie had always privately called floppy old-lady arms, and a neck with several chins. It wore a necklace that the flesh-and-blood woman must have bought in skinnier times, because the string between the pearls was stretched close to the breaking point. Apparently shadows worry about losing weight, too, because it was having a salad.

It asked Fernie, "What's your name, dear?"

"Fernie What."

Endearing herself to Fernie by not immediately doing the *Fernie what?* thing, the shadow woman gave her the warmest of all possible smiles and said, "It's a genuine delight to meet you, Fernie. I'm Gustav's great-aunt Mellifluous, and I've always wanted Gustav to have a playmate of his own kind."

Fernie almost told Gustav's great-aunt Mellifluous that she and Gustav weren't really playmates, at least not yet, because none of what they'd done together so far fit anybody's definition of *play*. "Thank you, ma'am. I don't mean to hurry you, but my cat—"

"Did just run by," Great-Aunt Mellifluous said, "and did scamper off into one of those hallways behind us."

Fernie wasn't looking forward to chasing Harrington down another endless hallway but supposed that it couldn't be helped. "I should get after him then."

"However," Great-Aunt Mellifluous said, hurrying to get it in before Fernie and Gustav were out of sight, "I'm afraid I must ask you to give up on finding him tonight."

Fernie began, "But I don't want to go home without him—"

"Oh, I'm certain that you love your cat very much and that you're a responsible young girl who takes good care of her pet. Still, we know that he's somewhere in the house, and if you went home to bed where a girl your age should be this time of night, I'm sure that Gustav would be able to catch him within a day or two and look after the poor dear until the pair of you can be joyously reunited."

Fernie didn't want to give up just yet. "He could still get hurt."

"And so could you," Great-Aunt Mellifluous said gently.

Hearing an adult, even a shadow adult, point this out gave Fernie pause.

"I'm certain that he's a very nice cat," Great-Aunt Mellifluous continued, "maybe even the best cat you've ever known, but he could be the greatest cat who ever lived and you'd still be far more important to your family than he is. Trust me, dear, you don't want to be wandering around this place while the People Taker is loose."

"Gustav already rescued me from him once tonight," Fernie admitted.

A shadow man in some kind of red military uniform who was eating an entire shadow roast pig on the other side of the table, and getting the shadow gravy all over its long white shadow mustache, put down the entire roast hog it held in its hands and snapped, "Then you should know that he's dark and cruel and dangerous and has no problem with *taking* a little girl down to the Dark Country and handing her over to Lord Obsidian to live forever as his cannon fodder."

Fernie had to agree that this wasn't something she was at all likely to enjoy. She was about to ask the most pressing of all the questions she'd been carrying around—who this Lord Obsidian was—when she noticed something that took her breath away, in its own way as amazing as anything else she'd seen so far.

Two high-backed wooden chairs had appeared on either side of Great-Aunt Mellifluous. The table itself had stretched to make room for them, teeming plates of shadow foods popping up at the new place settings. A pair of very recognizable shadows, one a young boy and one a young girl, had leaped out of nowhere to claim those seats and were even now devouring their meal with great abandon.

The shadow boy, who looked just like Gustav, was having food Fernie didn't recognize at all.

The shadow girl seemed to be having pizza. Its shadow legs didn't end where they touched the floor, but instead stretched farther, a pair of straight gray lines reaching past the back of the chair and several feet across the carpet to where they became a pair of shadow feet in shadow Frankenstein's monster—head slippers, touching the real Frankenstein's monster—head slippers on the real Fernie's feet.

Fernie would have jumped away when she realized just whose shadow this was, but it turned out that she couldn't move her legs.

CHAPTER NINE
FERNIE SAYS,
"YOUR HOUSE IS REALLY STUPID."

Up to this point, Fernie hadn't paid much attention to her own shadow or Gustav's. Somehow, with all the other shadows running around, she hadn't seen the point. She didn't know whether they had been following along all this time or taking breaks to run their own private errands.

Happily munching away at her shadow pizza, Fernie's shadow looked just like Fernie herself would have looked eating pizza, except that both the pizza and the girl were gray and smoky things that could be seen through. In fact, it looked familiar for reasons other than its resemblance to Fernie. For the first time, Fernie realized that it was the very same girl, or shadow girl, who had defended her from the Beast in the house's library.

Great-Aunt Mellifluous followed Fernie's

stare to her shadow self, who was at that moment accidentally letting some hot shadow tomato sauce spill onto her shadow pajamas. "Oh, dear," Great-Aunt Mellifluous said. "That's going to leave a spot."

Gustav, whose own shadow was still munching away at a meal that didn't look like anything Fernie had ever seen, told Fernie, "Look at it eat. You must have been hungry."

Fernie had been, and now that she stopped to think about it for a second, she remembered that it was pizza she'd been craving. "But the shadow's eating! I'm not!"

"Your shadow's eating *for* you," Gustav explained, "because you can't eat shadow food with a real mouth."

Fernie couldn't taste the pizza the shadow version of herself was eating, but she did feel her stomach getting fuller with every bite her shadow ate. "I didn't say it could eat for me!"

"You eat for it," Gustav said.

"But I can't eat shadow food!"

"And your shadow can't eat real food," Gustav replied, "but if you were home and ate so much that you got fat, wouldn't your shadow get fat, too?"

Fernie's mouth opened and closed without making any sound.

"And," Gustav continued, "if you stopped eating and got skinny, wouldn't your shadow get skinny, too?"

Fernie's mouth continued to open and close without any sound coming out. The revelation that every time in her life that she'd ever had a bowl of macaroni and cheese she'd been feeding not only herself but the dark shape that followed her around was so amazing that she knew she'd never eat macaroni and cheese again without being reminded with every bite that she was filling up not just her own stomach but another, darker one.

"My shadow always eats for me," Gustav said. "It's not like there's ever any real food in the house for me. There's no money here, and none of the shadows could ever go shopping even if there was."

Fernie considered that tremendously sad, but that wasn't what bothered her right now, not with her feet both stuck to the floor as if nailed there. "How come Snooks's shadow can step away from him and run around by itself and Harrington's shadow can step away from him and run around by itself and even Mr. Notes's shadow can step away from him and run around by itself, but mine won't let me walk away from this spot?"

"That is odd," Gustav agreed, a look of worry on his serious face. "I can walk away from mine. Just look."

He stepped away from the two shadow legs of his shadow self and strutted around in circles, while the shadow Gustav, completely unbothered by his antics, continued to devour its shadow meal.

Fernie tried again, just in case she'd been doing something wrong. But as much as she tugged, her feet remained planted where they were, attached to her shadow feet.

Great-Aunt Mellifluous said, "I must admit, that's one of the strangest things I've ever seen."

Fernie grabbed her right leg with both arms and pulled with all her strength. It remained stuck to the floor. "You mean to say that you've never seen anything like this before?"

"Never," Great-Aunt Mellifluous said. "Shadows all over your world may be able to decide whether they want to stay with their people or leave them behind, but I've never at any point in my shadow life seen one that could hold its human in place. Maybe because I've never seen one that wanted to." It turned to the shadow girl. "You're being rude. Let Fernie go."

The shadow Fernie swallowed its latest bite of pizza and spoke in a voice that sounded just like the real Fernie's, only grayer and angrier. "When I'm done eating."

"I said *now*," Great-Aunt Mellifluous commanded.

The shadow Fernie rolled its eyes and threw down its shadowy pizza slice, which instantly turned into gray smoke and sank back into the surface of the table like a thrown rock sinking into the surface of a pond. The shadow girl disappeared as well, or at least went off someplace where it could sulk in privacy.

Fernie lifted one slippered foot off the floor and then the other, relieved at being able to move her legs again. The drawback, of course, was that she didn't cast a shadow right now—and that felt every bit not right.

When she turned to Gustav and Great-Aunt Mellifluous to see what they had to say about this, she found the pair exchanging alarmed looks.

Gustav grabbed her by the wrist. "Come on. We have to get you home."

His sudden urgency so completely took Fernie by surprise that she didn't protest until they'd left the banquet behind and were well along one of the branching corridors, a downward-slanting hallway so steep that running in that direction amounted to little more than controlled falling. By the time Fernie got mad and yanked her arm away from Gustav's grip, the slope had grown even steeper, and the marble floor even more slippery. The only safe thing to do was to treat it like a slide. She fell on her backside next to where Gustav had fallen on his backside and joined him in plunging down the hall while the doors on both sides raced by too quickly to be seen.

They slid for so very long that Fernie had to think that they were now far, far underground, if not at the center of the Earth then at least far deeper than any basement had any right to be, unless there were top secret government weapons or a villain's secret laboratory in it.

Fernie shouted, "Is this your idea of a shortcut?"

Gustav yelled back, "What's wrong with it?"

The hallway started leveling out, but Fernie and Gustav were moving too fast to stop. Fernie looked ahead and saw the hallway seeming to end at what looked like a big picture window two stories above the street. The new Fluorescent Salmon house of the What family could be clearly seen in the bright glow of the streetlights, even if the black lines of the Gloom mansion's iron fence made it look like it had been cut into narrow slices.

As much as she wanted to get home, Fernie did not particularly relish the idea of a shortcut that required her to crash through a plate-glass window. So she yelled, *"Gustav!"*

And he yelled, *"Whaaaaaaaat?"* which might have been him calling her name or might have been the more common kind of *what*.

For a heartbeat, the picture window loomed so close that Fernie braced herself for the sound of shattering glass.

Then the view of the street seemed to lift out of sight like a curtain raised at the last moment. The long slide of a hallway had ended in a sudden drop just short of that picture window, leaving the two kids to fall head over heels into darkness.

Fernie had just enough time to wonder if this was the Pit he'd mentioned before she landed in something spongy and bounced up and down a little before coming to a stop. She almost mistook the surface beneath her for a trampoline or a pile of pillows or something like that, until she stirred some of it by moving her hand around and saw that it was a great big mound of shadow-stuff, about four times her own height and just solid enough to provide a soft landing.

When she glanced back up at the place she and Gustav had fallen from, she found that she could make out the end of the hallway they'd just slid down, which looked like a square pipe hanging in midair that curved upward until it disappeared in distant murk. A couple of puffs of darkness billowed from the open end and began to tumble downward toward her.

Fernie suddenly understood something she wished she hadn't. "That was a garbage chute."

"Well, yes," Gustav replied as if it should have been obvious. "Everybody has to clear their places when they're finished eating."

"But it was the size of a hallway, and it had doors along the walls. Why would there be doors you couldn't even get to without sliding down the garbage chute?"

"Not everybody in the family's lucky enough to get the best bedroom." He grabbed her by the wrist again and said, "Come on, we need to hurry. If we run through the Gallery of Awkward Statues and the Too Much Sitting Room, we'll make it back to the parlor, and—"

Suddenly irritated at him for not giving her any time to think, Fernie yanked her arm away from his and fought her way out of the big mound of shadow garbage on her own. Though for her it was only like struggling through slightly thicker air, she couldn't stop herself from wondering if any shadow person would think it smelled bad.

When she was finished climbing down, she stepped out onto solid floor and was able to look around. The area around them was a vast, open, and mostly empty space from which it was possible to look up and see many other hallways and chambers of the Gloom household. Some of the hallways zigzagged, some looped around one another like ribbons, and some went in directions that hurt her eyes to look at.

Although the mound of shadow garbage was highest where she and Gustav had landed, the gray-black mist remained ankle-deep where she now stood and billowed up in a little puffy cloud when she shifted her slippered foot.

Gustav arrived next to her and asked, "You ready to go?"

She gave him a sour look. "You know what? Your house is really stupid."

"At least it's not painted Fluorescent Salmon."

She had no immediate answer to that.

"Come on," he said, reaching for her wrist again. "The People Taker can be anywhere. We have to—"

She pulled free and crossed her arms. "You can take me through the Too Much Sitting Room, or whatever else comes next, after you tell me why we had to run away from the banquet in such a hurry."

"We don't have time. You might be in terrible danger right now."

"I might be," she agreed, her arms still stubbornly crossed, "but I don't think I'll be in any *more* danger than I am, and probably a lot less, if I understand what's going on."

Gustav's grunt was similar to the noise Fernie's dad made whenever Fernie wanted a reason she couldn't stay up another half hour to watch the end of a scary movie. *Because I said so* had never worked as an argument in the What household, no matter how often he said it. He said, "Your shadow was able to keep you from moving."

"So? Your great-aunt Mellifluous yelled at it and made it let me go."

"It still shouldn't have been able to do that."

Fernie looked at Gustav's face. It was the same serious face she had seen through the fence, the same serious face that had been her constant companion and, she had to admit, good friend for the last couple of hours . . . but there was something new in his eyes that she hadn't seen before.

Fear.

CHAPTER TEN
THE GALLERY OF AWKWARD STATUES

Gustav Gloom didn't have the time to stop and explain, but it would take less time than not stopping to explain. So he spoke quickly.

"That shadow I mentioned before, Lord Obsidian? He's not satisfied with shadows having a world of their very own and a few houses like this in your world. He wants to conquer the Dark Country, declare himself king, then invade your world and take over. He won't be satisfied until shadows walk around like people, and all the people of the world are dragged along the ground after them like shadows."

Fernie had to admit that didn't sound like much fun at all. At the very least, it would be hard to stay clean. "But how was any of that made worse by what happened upstairs?"

"Before now, he would have wanted the People Taker to get you just because he wants prisoners and slaves. But once your shadow showed that she was able to keep you from moving, you became something he could *learn from*, something that can teach him what he needs to know in order to get what he wants. We have to get you out of this house and back home before he can find you."

Fernie hugged herself for warmth even though the air around them was neither warm nor cold. "You'll keep looking for Harrington?"

Gustav looked offended. "I wouldn't dream of not continuing to look for Harrington."

Fernie did something she didn't expect to do: She wrapped him in a tight hug.

Gustav took to being hugged about as well as a tree would, except that a tree would not have given the impression that it might have preferred to run away. Nor would any tree have made as many attempts to figure out what to do with its arms.

Come to think of it, Gustav didn't take to being hugged even *nearly* as well as a tree would.

Fernie released him, wiped her eyes, and said, "Okay. The way out. What comes next? The Too Much Sitting Room?"

"First the Gallery of Awkward Statues and

then the Too Much Sitting Room and *then* just one flight of stairs to the parlor, where it's just a short walk to the front door."

None of that sounded as bad as hallways that doubled as garbage chutes and misty bedrooms with shadow dinosaurs in them. "Okay."

They fell into an uncomfortable silence as they walked, Gustav thinking about whatever a boy raised by shadows thinks about, and Fernie wondering if she'd ever see her home again. Aside from all the corridors and rooms visible in the murk high above their heads, there didn't seem to be any walls in sight. The room was just an endless plain, knee-deep in swirling darkness, offering no obvious way out except for picking one featureless spot in the distance and heading for it in the hope that it might turn out to be a somewhat less featureless spot than the featureless spot where they were.

Gustav said, "There's the first one."

He pointed at a mountainous white shape, still little more than a speck in the distance.

"That looks about ten miles away," Fernie complained.

"I know," Gustav said, "but it's really not as big as it looks." Just to prove his point, he leaned over, plucked the white speck off the ground with his thumb and forefinger, and tossed it over his shoulder.

This made Fernie's head hurt about as much as everything else that had happened in Gustav's house put together.

They continued walking. Another white speck appeared in the distance, this one growing larger and fatter and more clearly not just a speck as Fernie and Gustav approached it.

Before long it revealed itself as a sculpture—and not just any sculpture, but one of those massive, looming, white marble sculptures of a heroic-looking, muscle-bound man. Fernie had seen a number of sculptures like that in museums and in movies set in museums, and had always been impressed by the way the figures in the sculptures were constantly doing noble things like waving swords or standing at podiums making speeches or holding the Earth over their heads.

This one, though, didn't look nearly as important.

The statue depicted a man, as muscle-bound as a mythical hero, stooping to examine the sole of his right foot to see whether he'd stepped in something.

It was such a realistic marble sculpture that Fernie could tell that he had. It wasn't just that it looked gooshy and smeary, but his stone face was also contorted with disgust at the smell.

"Ewww," said Fernie, pleased.

"It's one of my favorites," Gustav agreed.

They walked on. The shadowy mist covering the ground started to lift, gradually revealing a floor of white and black tiles. More statues appeared. There were dozens of them, and then hundreds. They all seemed as solid as real statues, even if they were only the shadows of statues that had never been. Most of them were white like marble, but others had the gray or green look of statues cast in metal. None of them were striking heroic or noble or even thoughtful poses, but were instead frozen in place doing things that most statues in museums would rather die than be caught doing.

There were statues of people sneezing, statues of people scratching their elbows, and statues of people picking their noses. There were many statues of people who might have been fine subjects for statues had they not been caught with their eyes half closed and with their mouths half open, less like sculptures than snapshots taken at the wrong fraction of a second.

Fernie understood. "It's like the library. The books in that place are all the shadows of ideas nobody ever had. These are all the shadows of statues that nobody ever bothered to sculpt."

"I don't know why," Gustav said. "I like them."

"They're not exactly the kind of statues you find in museums, though."

"I wouldn't know," he said with the boredom of a boy who had never been to one.

"Do you also have a separate room of music that nobody ever bothered to play?"

"Of course not," Gustav sniffed. "That would be just plain silly."

This struck Fernie as the strangest thing he had said all night. "Why would that be sillier than anything else?"

Gustav didn't seem to have an answer to that one. "I don't know. It just would be."

"Maybe it's a room you haven't seen yet," she said.

He shrugged.

"Or maybe," she said, struck by a sudden brainstorm, "there's a room like that in the shadow house in Liechtenstein."

"Or the one in Orlando," he supposed.

Soon the statues around them numbered in the thousands, stretching away as far as the eye could see.

This brought up something else Fernie had been having trouble figuring out. "Just so I know, are these all real statues or shadow statues? Are all the books in the library and the furniture in the parlor real things or shadow things?"

Gustav said, "Both, I guess. It's complicated. All I really understand is that these are things that could have been real in the world outside . . . but never were. Inside the house, they're as real as they need to be." They continued walking for a while.

Fernie would have loved to take her time appreciating all the great sculptures of historical generals with crossed eyes and brilliant scientists finding stones in their shoes, but then Gustav's mood changed again. He sped up, pressing forward with the kind of haste he'd shown only in emergencies. Fernie had to walk faster just to keep up with him. "What's wrong?"

"I'm beginning to suspect that coming this way might not have been such a good idea."

She started to jog. "What? Why not?"

"Because it really does *look* an *awful lot* like it wasn't such a good idea."

This didn't give Fernie any more useful information than she'd had before, but something about the fear on Gustav's pale little face made her press the point, even as he broke into a full-out run and she found herself having to do the same. Her Frankenstein's monster–head slippers fell off behind her, probably lost forever. "Why not?"

"Because it *wasn't* a good idea!" he cried.

By then they were both pumping their arms and driving their legs as hard as they could. Fernie breathed in ragged gasps as the silent figures of the Gallery of Awkward Statues became mute, stupidly positioned blurs on both sides. They sped past statues of men shaving and of dogs sniffing the hind parts of other dogs and of armless women staring cross-eyed at the flies that had landed on the tips of their noses.

Fernie finally willed herself to look back over her shoulder to see what they were running *from*.

It was several hundred feet behind them, a little island of absolute darkness, brandishing its claws and spines and pincers and even more terrible things as it hopped from the shoulders of a statue of President Nixon cleaning his ear with a cotton swab to the shoulders of a statue of President Lincoln sucking on a spoon. The violence of its landing shattered the President Lincoln statue from the waist up. Shadow marble dust billowed outward in a cloud. A terrible black shape at the darkness's center leaped again, its fanged mouth gaping so wide that the rest of its body seemed hardly large enough to justify the opening.

It was the creature from the library.

It was the Beast.

CHAPTER ELEVEN
AN AWKWARD LIBERTY

"This way!"

Gustav darted to his left so abruptly that Fernie almost missed the turn. She skidded on the tile floor and almost went down, but recovered and followed him around a statue depicting a bunch of embarrassed Civil War soldiers removing a mama cat and her kittens from the mouth of a cannon. They were barely ten paces past that statue when they heard another statue shatter to pieces behind them.

"Again!" Gustav yelled and led Fernie around a rather impressive sculpture, this one the famous image of five marines and a sailor planting the American flag in Iwo Jima. In this version the marine in front was hollering bloody murder because the others had jabbed the tip of the flagpole into his foot.

Another huge crash followed as this sculpture

also shattered into hundreds of pieces.

The Beast was powerful, the Beast was fast, and the Beast was dangerous, but the Beast wasn't the most patient creature in the world. It wasn't much for taking the time to go around obstacles. It seemed it could smash through anything and certainly enjoyed doing so . . . even though fighting its way clear of the wreckage slowed it down.

Unfortunately, running around the biggest and heaviest sculptures to keep placing them in the Beast's path slowed Fernie and Gustav down even more.

"This isn't working!" Fernie cried.

"I know! But I have a plan!"

This was more than Fernie had at the moment, so she just bit her lip and concentrated on running.

Fernie felt a whoosh of air right behind her tug at the back of her pajamas and heard the sound of ripping cloth as unseen shadow claws cut slashes in the loose fabric of her pajama top. She knew the Beast would get her before she ran even one more step. This was not the library, after all. She was not standing close to any walls with any sliding panels that might reveal a friend eager to pull her into any secret passages.

The most she could do was yell "Duck!" and throw herself to the ground.

Gustav obeyed, and the massive black shape of the Beast sailed by just over their heads, smashing face-first into the sculpture that they'd been about to use for cover. It became a cloud of dust and so did the sculpture ten feet behind it and the sculpture ten feet behind that. The Beast was apparently so slow to figure out that it had accidentally left Gustav and Fernie behind that it smashed another half dozen of the sculptures in a straight line before it doubled back.

"That," Fernie managed, "just might be the very stupidest monster on the planet."

Gustav was already back on his feet and pulling at Fernie's arm. "It'll be back on us in no time. Hurry!"

They ran again, this time in another direction. The sound of smashing marble grew faint in the distance behind them . . . and then grew louder again.

Fernie started to wonder if the answer was going to be continuing to throw herself to the floor every single time the Beast leaped. Sure, she thought, it had worked once, but it was far from the kind of thing somebody could just keep doing indefinitely, even if the Beast was dumb enough to keep falling for it.

And then she looked past the next twenty rows of statues at a great familiar shape she had been too busy to see as anything but a wall and knew where Gustav was leading her. It was an awkward shadow version of one of the biggest statues of all.

This was a Statue of Liberty that nobody had ever seen while sailing into New York Harbor.

This Liberty was scratching an unbearable itch on her right hip. Her robe was all bunched up around her waist as she gathered enough fabric with her left hand to give her right hand access to the affected spot. Nor was that the only itchy place: She was also using the heel of her left foot to rub what looked like a manhole cover–size mosquito bite on her right ankle.

To free her hands, she had tucked her engraved tablet and the handle of her burning torch under her right armpit; and, true to what would have happened to anybody itchy enough to do something so careless with a flame, she'd accidentally set the fabric around her shoulders on fire. Wrought-iron flames, glowing from internal lamps, rose from that part of her as well. Her expression suggested that she didn't realize that she was on fire, as she was too distracted with reaching her terrible itch. Her struggle with her robes was so intense that her crown sat crookedly on her head, sliding downward to her right side and revealing a host of loose, frizzy hairs made of what looked like iron pipes.

It looked like she needed a very big comb.

Fernie remembered learning in school that the real Statue of Liberty had been a gift from France to the United States. Even as she ran toward this never-imagined version, her life depending on whatever Gustav had in mind, part of her wondered just what America's reaction would have been had France offered this one instead. And if it had been built? Generations of poor immigrants, huddled together on ships from Europe, might have taken one look at the giant figure in the harbor . . . and decided to go back.

All of this went through Fernie's mind in less than a second. But then an enraged roar, not far enough behind her, reminded her that she and Gustav had far more terrible things to worry about. "It's coming!"

"I know! Just run!"

Expecting the terrible grasp of the Beast at any moment, Fernie pushed herself to run harder and concentrated on the feet of the silly Lady Liberty, which were right now the most important feet in the world.

Just ahead of her, Gustav ran past the one sandaled foot that was flat on the ground, and veered behind it. Seeing what he was up to, but not knowing if she would get there in time, she risked one last look over her shoulder and saw the Beast, closer than she ever would have feared, looming like a patch of darkness between her and the rest of the world.

Again it grabbed for her. Again she threw herself to the ground, and again she caught a glimpse of something dark and terrible, something that didn't seem to have any particular shape, sailing past her, right over her head. She turned to follow its path and saw it hit the shadow Liberty at just the spot where the giant lady used the heel of one foot to scratch an itch on the other.

There was a tremendous crash. She saw the Beast's legs sticking out of a crater at the spot where the two giant legs crossed. She heard it bellow as it realized it was stuck and watched as it tore another huge gouge in the plate metal to free itself.

Not far away, Gustav yelled, "Run!"

Fernie got up and ran with what felt like the last of her strength, but only for a little bit, because the terrible creaking sound had already started and she wasn't able to stop herself from turning around to see the collapse.

The statue's giant legs were no longer able to stay up after the damage the Beast had done to the crossed ankles. With a tremendous ripping and crashing and snapping of metal, it started to fall in on itself. The upper reaches of the statue fell and collapsed all the smaller ones. They sank as if a bottomless hole had opened up . . . except that there was no hole in the floor and the only thing the statue could fall into was itself.

The last thing to hit was the awkward Liberty's head, which retained its look of distracted concentration until it had nowhere else to fall. Then it fell apart, too, in a cloud of dust.

It would have been breathtaking if Fernie had had any breath to take. As it was, she just felt her own knees buckle and sank to the ground.

"Wow," she managed.

Gustav waved at her as he came around the hill of twisted metal. His black suit was covered in dust, but otherwise he looked fine—like a boy who hadn't just been chased by a monster.

As he drew close, Fernie asked him, "Is it dead?"

"Unfortunately," Gustav Gloom said, "you can't kill a shadow by flattening it."

Fernie thought about that and said, "I guess you couldn't. They're flat already."

"On the other hand, being buried by tons of shadow statue should put this one down for a little while."

"How much of a while?"

Gustav performed some mental calculations. After a few seconds he held his thumb and forefinger about an inch apart. "A *little* while."

"That little, huh?"

He examined just how far apart his two fingertips were and after some more consideration, moved them a little bit closer together. "No. Maybe *this* little."

Some of the smaller pieces on the surface of the wreckage shifted. Was it because they were still settling from the fall, or because something dark and dangerous underneath the pile was digging its way out? "You don't happen to have any other big statues around here in case we need to bury it again?"

"I know of one even larger. It's four heads carved into the side of a mountain, all of them with very serious expressions except for the bearded man, who's sneezing. I suppose that if we could get the whole mountain to collapse on the Beast all at once, we might be able to imprison it for a long time."

"Then let's do that," Fernie suggested.

"Unfortunately, the mountain's also a long way from here and not in the direction we're headed. Besides, I'm not sure I have any idea how we'd go about bringing down a whole mountain. It probably isn't even possible."

Fernie realized that the last thing she wanted to do was make burying and reburying the Beast a lifelong job. "How about we just return to getting me out of the house? How far is this Too Much Sitting Room?"

"Not far. We got a little sidetracked just now, but we should be there in a few minutes if we walk quickly."

"Sounds like a plan," she said.

CHAPTER TWELVE
THE TOO MUCH SITTING ROOM

Fernie didn't ask Gustav how the Too Much Sitting Room could possibly be anywhere nearby when the Gallery of Awkward Statues seemed to stretch for miles in every direction and there weren't any walls in sight, let alone doors. She just assumed by this point that Gustav knew where he was going.

This turned out to be true, and the border between one room and the next had nothing to do with walls or doors or hallways. If you stood in one place, the gallery seemed to go on forever. But if you walked in a certain direction following somebody who knew the way, the awkward sculptures started to fade out and a dark, dusty little room lined with books and wooden paneling and filled with overstuffed, high-backed comfy chairs started to fade in to replace it.

Many of the chairs were occupied by silent, unmoving people who had sank partway into the big plush cushions. They all looked like real people, not shadows, but though none of them looked dead, none of them looked like they were ever going to get out of their chairs anytime soon. A burning fire in a nearby hearth made it hard to blame them for staying put, as everything about the room made it look like a perfect place for a nice, long sit, even if *nice* and *long* were just different words for *forever and ever.*

Before the last of the awkward sculptures faded all the way out and the last of the comfy chairs faded all the way in, Gustav warned Fernie not to sit down, no matter how tired her legs were from all the running, or how inviting the chairs looked.

Fernie suddenly felt the need to say, "I think I owe you an apology."

"For what?"

"For saying that your house is stupid."

Gustav shrugged. "Sometimes it is stupid. Sometimes your world is stupid."

"I didn't mean to apologize for *thinking* that your house was stupid. I meant to apologize for *saying* it. That was rude. Friends don't treat each other that way."

This left Gustav silent for a long time. "Is that what we are?"

Fernie said, "Aren't we?"

He thought about it. "I was hoping we could be. I've never really had a friend before."

"Come on. That can't be true. What about your family? Mr. Notes? They all seemed pretty friendly."

Gustav struggled with what seemed like a difficult explanation. "They try," he said finally. "I was raised by one very good shadow who isn't around anymore, and I guess you would call her my friend if you can count the person who acts as your mother as a friend. There are some like Great-Aunt Mellifluous who also do what they can to love me and take care of me, and I love them back, but being with them, being friends with them, doesn't feel like being with people. It's more like being with the idea of a person, if you know what I mean. Which can sometimes be even more lonely."

"But there are so many of them. Millions, maybe. How could you possibly be lonely when there are so many?"

Gustav hesitated again. It seemed that some things were hard to speak out loud, if only because that meant looking at them.

"Most of the others don't really talk to me. They don't mean me any harm, but they don't think I belong here and don't care all that much whether I live or die. They don't care whether anybody lives or dies. It's the same reason that somebody like the People Taker can just move in, coming and going whenever he wants, snatching people out in your world and bringing them here for Lord Obsidian's pleasure. Because they don't think it's any of their business."

"That's pretty mean of them," Fernie said.

"It's natural, I guess. It really doesn't have much to do with them, so they don't think about it much."

After a moment, she said, "Do you always have to run from monsters?"

"The Beast's not the first one, if that's what you mean. He's not even the worst."

"It must be scary living here."

"Sometimes. But it's like I told you: I'm used to it. I guess that's another reason why I never really tried to do anything about the People Taker before he snatched all those people on your side of the fence. It just didn't seem all that unusual to me. Monsters, people takers, beasts, dangerous rooms . . . they're all just things I've grown up with."

There wasn't much she could say about that, either. He gave the impression that he'd realized this would be a part of his life for as long as Fernie was around and that he knew he might as well learn how to deal with it properly.

"Either way," Gustav said, "having a human friend is going to change things, I think."

Fernie gave his arm a comforting squeeze. He didn't seem to do any better with that than he had with the hug. But he didn't pull away, either.

They walked farther. The last of the awkward statues faded. The Too Much Sitting Room grew sharper and more distinct until it was suddenly the only place visible around them. It was now possible to see that many of the motionless people in the chairs were covered with dust and cobwebs, even though in many cases their eyes were open and watching Fernie and Gustav hurry by. Most looked resentful. A few, a very few, mumbled to themselves, giving the impression that whatever conversation they thought they were having had been going around in circles for far longer than anybody on Sunnyside Terrace had been alive.

Fernie, who was not only hours past her usual bedtime but, after all, wearing pajamas, found herself yawning and thinking about how nice it would be to sink into one of these big chairs, if only for a moment. It was not a great thought to have, but there it was in her head as if the room had found a fine unoccupied shelf somewhere between her ears and *put* it there. She shivered. "Why doesn't the People Taker take *these* people? It's not like they'd run away."

"He wouldn't be able to lift any of them," Gustav said. "Once you sit in any of these chairs, you become part of it forever. These people are just . . . upholstery, who can think and see and remember being people and wish they could move."

She gulped. "Can they speak?"

"Yes, but you don't want to talk to them. All they ever do is suggest that you pull up a chair and make yourself comfortable."

This was somehow even worse. "Why would there even be a room like this in your house? I understand the library and the gallery, but what does something like this have to do with shadows?"

"The way Great-Aunt Mellifluous once explained it to me is that people who spend their entire lives sitting around never doing anything become shadows of what they could have been, so they deserve a room here as much as anybody."

Fernie chewed on this for a bit. She didn't like it from any angle. "I kind of want to take back my apology for calling this house stupid."

"I thought you might," Gustav said, without taking any particular offense.

The pair hurried past the various circles of high-backed chairs where sleepy and motionless and despairing figures sat slumped with nothing to do but stare at one another. Some, driven by boredom or malice, called to the two children, noting that they looked tired and that they really ought to get off their feet.

"The stairs are over there," Gustav said, pointing to a black door between one of the fireplaces and a sizable painting of a comfortable chair empty but for a single forlorn hand reaching for freedom from some hopeless prison beneath sofa cushions. "One flight up's the grand parlor, which you've already seen, and once we're there all we have to do is get you back to the entrance hall and out the front door."

The grand parlor would be a relief. The talking shadows had scared her on the way in, but they wouldn't be so terrible now that she knew what they were and had spoken to a couple.

She knew she had Gustav to thank for getting this far, and was about to say so when he stopped so short that she almost collided with his back. What Fernie had mistaken for just another patch of darkness on the floor now turned out to be the People Taker, squatting with his back against the door as he waited for Fernie and Gustav to draw close.

Gustav had said that the People Taker was as human as she was, but when he drew himself to his feet, he was like a column of greasy black smoke rising from some unseen, burning place. An evil, happy grin spread across his pale skin, cracking his face in two. Fernie could imagine him grinning that same grin while doing all manner of cruel and malicious things to all of the people he'd *taken*.

"Ffffernie," he exclaimed with what seemed genuine delight. "Gustavvvvv. I ssssssent my pet into the gallery to fetch you. How tricky you mussssst have been to get this far!"

Gustav kept himself between Fernie and the People Taker. "We were tricky, all right. We buried him."

"Did you now?" The People Taker chuckled. "Mussssst have been enjoyable fffffor you. I've buried lotsssss of people, and I've *never* gotten tired of it."

He took a single, unhurried step. It was clearly the walk of a living, breathing, solid, flesh-and-blood man, but he was also clearly as much a creature of absolute darkness as anything Fernie had seen in this house. He seemed to swallow the surrounding light with every step, putting it out as simply as most people can put out a candle by snuffing the wick between thumb and forefinger.

For the first time, Fernie noticed that for such a dark presence, he didn't seem to have a shadow himself. That reminded Fernie that Gustav had hurried her away from her own back in the banquet room, and she turned to check whether it was with her again; and, yes, there it was on the ground, trembling with fear and candlelight.

Gustav Gloom stepped away from him,

forcing Fernie to retreat the same distance. "You've never been able to *take* me. You've been trying for months but haven't ever gotten close. And you won't ever get to *take* Fernie, either. I'll stop you if you try."

The People Taker wagged a finger. "Ssssssilly boy. Whoever said I could be sssssstopped?"

He moved. In all her life, Fernie had never seen any man move faster. In an instant, his clutching, pale, white hands became missiles, dragging the impossibly long coal-black sleeves of his arms behind them.

Before Fernie even knew what had happened, his gloved hands had closed tight around Gustav's neck.

Or at least they would have if Gustav hadn't moved.

Instead, the cold fingers closed on empty air.

In the same insanely brief instant, Gustav had shoved Fernie aside and dodged the People Taker's grasp. Fernie cried an indignant protest as she fell but, even before she hit the floor, had time to appreciate the look of even greater surprise on the People Taker's face as his hands closed all the way into fists without ever encountering a neck.

The People Taker's dark eyes fixed themselves on Gustav and memorized exactly where he'd gone.

One more impossibly fast lunge later, the terrible fists once again closed on empty air, just short of Gustav's throat.

"You're fffffast," the People Taker noted.

"I was raised by shadows," Gustav replied. "Have you ever tried to catch one?"

An awful sound, like broken glass crunching into smaller pieces when a boot steps on it, started in the People Taker's throat. Only the grin on the People Taker's face made it possible to recognize it as the sound he used for deep, uproarious laughter. "Would you like to know why I'm sssssstill sssssmiling?"

"Not particularly," Gustav said.

"I'm sssssmiling . . . because there's a diffffference between how fffffast I usually have to move . . . and how fffffast I *can* move."

The People Taker lunged again . . . and this time, when the fingers of his left hand closed, they found an actual neck to grasp. He lifted Gustav high off the ground with nothing but the strength of his left arm and stood there laughing while Gustav dangled, clawing at his fingers.

As terrible as his laughter was, he really did sound like he was having a good time.

Then the laughter ended and was replaced by a cry of pain. He wasn't having anything like a good time anymore.

As much attention as the People Taker had needed to pay to the strange little boy who had refused to allow himself to be *taken*, he had completely forgotten to pay attention to the little girl who the little boy had been protecting. And that little girl had belly-crawled across the floor and sunk her teeth into the spot where the hem of his right trouser leg had risen up and revealed an inch or so of pale, white ankle.

His ankle tasted much worse than she ever would have expected. Beneath a thin layer of dirt and sweat lay another taste so disgusting that it left her wondering how much of his life he had spent wading through troughs of mangled, rotten fish guts. But Fernie was determined to keep biting. She grabbed his foot and his leg and held on, even as the People Taker hollered in pain.

She almost allowed herself to hope that she and Gustav were winning.

And then the People Taker, faced with the need to do something with the boy in his hand so he could take care of the girl at his feet, did something terrible that Fernie hadn't considered at all.

He threw Gustav away.

Fernie happened to see Gustav's face as he sailed backward, reaching out with both arms. His eyes, meeting hers, were filled with apologies, saying more than any number of words ever would have been able to.

He landed in the seat of one of the empty high-backed chairs.

His arms and legs fell into place a fraction of a second later, his hands landing palms-down on the armrests.

He did not get up.

He didn't even turn his head, which had hit the seat back and must have become part of it at once. But a terrible, despairing expression appeared on his face. He cried out, "Fernie!"

Fernie screamed, "Gustav!"

This was a mistake, as screaming meant releasing her jaw's grip on the People Taker's ankle, and while biting his ankle now seemed like a tremendously lame way to fight him, it was also the only idea she'd had. Before she knew it, cold, dead fingers grabbed the collar of her pajamas and yanked her to her feet.

"That," the People Taker whispered, "was an unfffffortunate accident. I didn't mean that to happen at all."

"Liar!" Fernie screamed. "You—"

His other hand clamped tight around her jaw, holding it shut. His thumb and forefinger tightened on her nostrils, cutting off her air and leaving her unable to breathe.

"I'm ssssserious," the People Taker said, almost apologetically. "I wanted to *take* both of you. You were the last two I needed to make my quota. Now your fffffriend's stuck in that chair fffforever and I can't *take* him at all. It's a terrible inconvenience to me. Maybe you have a suggestion . . ."

He released Fernie's jaw. She gasped, swallowed a deep breath of air, and thrashed, feeling a little piece of herself die inside as her most powerful kick merely brushed against his ribs with a soft and embarrassing thump. *"Let me go!"*

The People Taker cocked his head to one side. "An interesting idea. Not one I would have sssssuggested, but an interesting idea nevertheless. Arguably, I *could* let you go, apologize, lead you out the fffffront door, let you go back home, and never bother you again. Jussssst out of the goodness of my heart or fffffor the sheer novelty of doing something difffffferent for a change. Maybe ifffff I did, my night would not be so awfully . . . predictable."

What followed was five seconds of the eeriest silence Fernie had ever known as the People Taker pretended to weigh the pros and cons of her idea.

Then he decided. "Naaaaahhhhh."

He took a satiny black bag out of a coat pocket and *took* her.

CHAPTER THIRTEEN
IT'S NOT TIME FOR PANCAKES

The People Taker turned out to be the kind of fellow who sang a happy tune as he went about his business.

With Fernie crammed inside his sack, he amused himself with a melody that might have been quite charming to anybody whose idea of music was the squeal car brakes emit when the wheels are skidding on ice.

Fernie did what she could to drown him out. She yelled for help and called him terrible names and told him that he was in big, big trouble and wept in fear. Then she decided that being angry was better than being terrified and went back to calling him names again.

None of this was at all useful, at least not as long as she was stuck inside this sack, smelling everybody else who'd ever been stuck in there before her. From what her nose told her, it must have been an awful lot of people, some of whom should have used deodorant.

After several minutes, he said, "Ahhhhh. We're *here*."

She heard him dialing a phone. This was hard to digest, not just because Gustav had said that there were no phones inside this house but also because it was impossible to imagine the People Taker having anybody to call. Who on earth could have wanted to answer a phone call from him?

She couldn't make out the conversation, but she could tell that it didn't sound at all like him. He didn't use his customary reptilian tones but spoke with a warm and friendly voice, concluding with a warm chuckle as he said good-bye.

The material around her loosened as he undid the drawstring. A pale light barely better than darkness streamed in just before he reached in and pulled Fernie out by the collar.

Holding her at arm's length, he whispered, "Loooook."

The large circular chamber around them had four equally spaced doorways, dingy gray walls, air so dusty that it burned her lungs, torches trying and failing to dispel the darkness with flickering light, and, at the center of it all, a floor that would have been like any other floor were it not interrupted by a black pit.

The Pit was circular and had a lower edge just over the side leading to another step down and then the deepest darkness Fernie had ever seen. It was impossible to see very far into what lay below as the gray mist that Fernie had come to recognize as concentrated shadow-stuff churned like a storm-tossed sea less than a foot down. But it was impossible to look at it and not know that it was bottomless.

The People Taker licked his lips. "That's the Pit."

"Duh," Fernie managed.

"Yesssss," the People Taker agreed, "I'm ssssssure you could already tell. It's a pit, and even if it is one of only ten pathways to the Dark Country in the entire world, there's ssssstill only a limited number of things it really could look like."

"Then why bother to tell me what it is?"

"Because I want you to understand. I'm *not* going to throw you in."

"You're not?"

"No, Ffffffernie, I have something better in

mind for you. But before you find out what, I'm going to tell you the terrible fate you'll be ssssspared, so you'll know how terrible the one awaiting you would have to be in order to be even worse. You sssssee, Ffffffernie, while shadows may have no problem using the Pit to travel back and forth from the Dark Country, people have a rougher time of it. Ffffffor people, it's just a long fall. A very long fall. It lasts longer than you could ever imagine. Hours. Days. Ssssssometimes weeks or months or years. It can last so long that you'll wonder if you'll die of old age before hitting the bottom. Then, when you land . . . you're ssssstuck in a strange and dangerous place, not at all ffffffriendly to human beings. You might wander there for a long time as I did when I fell . . . cold and helplesssss . . . with nobody to talk to and nobody to help you before Lord Obsidian finds you and makes you his ssssslave."

"It's still got to be better than being here with you!"

The People Taker's chuckle was like the rattle of a poisonous snake. "Oh, yesssss, dear Ffffffernie. It is. You're a smart girl. That's *exactly* the point I was making."

All of Fernie's grim determination to deny this evil man the satisfaction of seeing her beg for mercy nearly turned to water. She *almost* cried, *almost* wailed, *almost* told him that she'd do anything if he just let her go. She resisted, and that *almost* made her about as brave as any girl in her position could possibly be, but it didn't feel like bravery to her.

"Now," he said, "on to where you're going instead."

The People Taker tucked her under his arm and lugged her through a narrow opening. He proceeded along a winding hallway, up a long, curving flight of stairs, and through a number of stranger passages until he reached a smaller room empty except for an ancient high-backed wooden chair and a rickety table bearing an old-fashioned box-shaped thirteen-inch television. The TV had a V-shaped wire antenna and an empty hole where the picture tube should have been.

"I've never been much of a TV watcher," the People Taker remarked. "There's too much sssssinging, too much laughter, and I've never liked anything that sounds like people being"— his lip curled as he spoke the next word like a curse—"joyful. But this particular TV was a gift from my master. And it's *ssssspecial*. Wait till you see what it does."

He put her down. She couldn't see what he did to keep her in the chair, but when he let go and stepped away to address his attentions to the TV, she couldn't stand up or throw herself to the floor or do anything else to try to get away. It felt like having a rope around her neck, even though there were no ropes to speak of.

He played with the rabbit-ear antenna, making images appear where the screen should have been. Most of what came up were black-and-white images of places in the house, not just rooms she and Gustav had visited but places she hadn't, one of them an odd gallery of paintings that included the wedding portrait of a man who, from the resemblance, could have been Gustav's father, and a beautiful red-haired woman who must have been his mother. But that vanished, replaced by static, and the next image in line was an aerial view of the Beast limping away from the wreckage of the fallen Awkward Liberty.

As he worked the antenna, looking for the precise image he wanted, the People Taker chatted away. "After I fell into the Pit and landed where you would have landed, I sssspent more time wandering lost in the Dark Country than I like to think about. It's not a nice place, Fffffernie, not even for someone like me. There are things you can't sssssee that are far worse than the things you can."

"It sounds like the kind of place you deserve," Fernie said.

"That's what I thought," the People Taker agreed. "I began to wonder if I was being punished for all the bad things I'd done, all the people I'd *taken*. And I began to promise myself that if I ever got out, I'd be a better man." He paused. "That was, of course, a very sssssilly promise to make. I don't want to be a better man."

Fernie wasn't surprised. Not that it wouldn't have been nice for the People Taker to be a better man, but she had the distinct impression that he wouldn't have had the slightest clue how.

"So," he continued, "Lord Obsidian fffffound me and made me a special deal that he's never offfffered anybody else. He sssssaid that in exchange for my shadow, which he keeps beside him, he'd send me back to the world of people. For every nine people I *took* and threw into the Pit for him, I could keep one, just one, for my own personal amusement. You may have heard about all the ssssstrange disappearances in your town? I have been working toward my reward."

Fernie began to see what the People Taker had in mind for her that could be worse than throwing her into the Pit. "You said before that you only had two left to go."

"That's right. Just two. Which would normally mean the Pit for you. But you made it personal by hurting me. And I've had the most *wonderful* idea."

Fernie didn't ask him about his wonderful idea. When the People Taker said *wonderful*, he meant everything that was *not* wonderful. It meant bad things happening, one after another, long after it would have been fair for them to stop.

"This was my wonderful idea: What if I just keep you out of the way until I fffffind two others to give my master instead? It's a perfect sssssolution. He gets what he wants, and I get what I want. Everybody's happy."

"Except for me," Fernie said.

"Yesssss. You'll never be happy ever again.

You'll never be anything but afraid. But who's counting you?"

The picture on the screen changed again and again while he worked, revealing one room of the Gloom house after another. She saw a massive gong on a balcony, a glowing ball of fire hovering near a room with walls painted blue like the sky, an odd standing wardrobe with drawers that kept popping open and shut as dark, unfamiliar shapes leaped in and out, and a chandelier with thousands of black candles, each lit with something other than fire, which cast inky darkness instead of light.

And then he got the picture he wanted.

The empty space the TV had instead of a screen now showed the towering double doors at the entrance to the Gloom house. The light was grim and overcast, and the ground covered with the lawn's usual ankle-deep mist, but it was still clearly sometime after sunrise, and to Fernie's light-starved eyes it looked as bright as a day at the beach in the heart of summer.

The thought that she might not see anything as bright again, and might instead be spending the rest of a very short life in the company of the People Taker, was bad enough. But then the picture changed again and got much, much worse. Instead of being a picture of the Gloom family's front door, it became a picture of the What family's Fluorescent Salmon house, just as silly looking as it had been the day before, but now also the safest place in the entire world.

The front door opened.

Fernie's dad emerged, dressed in a blue suit with a red tie, followed by Pearlie in blue jeans and a black T-shirt with a picture of a giant dinosaur burning down a Japanese city. The T-shirt bore the words GODZILLA SURVIVOR.

"See?" the People Taker asked. "One, two. Exactly the number I need to give Lord Obsidian in order to get to keep you for myself."

Forgetting the invisible rope around her neck, Fernie cried out and tried to attack him. But the invisible bond held her tight.

Fernie's father and sister began to cross the street, the picture following them as they went, just like it would have if there had been a cameraman following them.

Grinning, the People Taker inquired, "Would you like to know what I said to him?"

He made a fist of his right hand and stuck out his thumb and pinky to turn the fist into a mock telephone. A dial tone emerged. He didn't dial—though it was clear that he could—but he did speak in the same gentle, likable, entirely human tones she had heard before while she was stuck in the sack and he was making his call. But this time his words weren't muffled at all. They were perfectly clear, and they were so far from being the sounds made by the People Taker that even though she could see him making them, she could also imagine the kind of man they should have come from: a chubby-cheeked, sweater-wearing neighbor with a cute little mustache and a swirl of thin hair on top of an otherwise shiny bald head.

"Hello? Is this Mr. What? . . . Mr. What, I'm Brad Gloom. I live across the street." He listened. "Yes, the big old house. I'm sorry for waking you up so early in the morning, but, gee, I didn't want you to worry. Fernie's okay." He listened some more. "No, I'm afraid you won't find her safe in her bed. It seems that your cat got loose late last night and she snuck out to go looking for him." Some more listening. "Well, you're right. As a father myself, I agree, it wasn't the safest or smartest thing in the world for her to do, but she's a little girl, and she loves her little cat. I can't blame her." A grin. "That's right, they're both over here, safe and sound. In fact, I made pancakes. Why don't you and *your other daughter come over here to join us? We'd love to meet you."*

He mimed hanging up the phone and grinned at her. On the TV, Fernie's father and sister passed the front gate of the Gloom estate and began to approach the front door.

Had desperation alone been enough to give Fernie the strength she needed, she would have ripped herself free of the invisible rope, smashed the chair into toothpicks, and hurled the People Taker against the nearest wall. "Don't you dare hurt them, you big . . ." There was no appropriate word. "I'll make you pay if you do."

He grinned. "I won't hurt them. They're not mine to hurt. My master, Lord Obsidian, will get to decide what to do with them. But you, Fffffernie . . . you *will* be mine."

On the screen, Fernie's father and sister arrived at the towering double doors of the Gloom mansion, which opened up for them. They peered inside, blinking at the darkness they saw within. Mr. What turned to Pearlie and said something Fernie couldn't hear, no doubt an expert opinion on the kinds of accidents that can befall unlucky people whose houses aren't adequately lit. Fernie couldn't hear Pearlie's answer, either, but it was easy enough to read the single word on her lips: *Whatever.*

Then they both entered, and the doors shut behind them.

"You know what?" the People Taker said. "I think I'm going to have fffffun with them. I think I'm going to actually let them go on thinking I'm going to make them pancakes. It'll make the moment when I throw them into the Pit that much more enjoyable. Why don't you watch and see how fffffunny it is."

Fernie screamed in rage and frustration, while the chuckling People Taker left to *take* her family.

Pancakes would surely not be involved.

CHAPTER FOURTEEN
THE PEOPLE TAKER MUST BE BRAD

The neighbors had always thought Gustav was the saddest little boy in the world. They thought this because he looked lonely behind the fence, and because he never seemed to smile, never seemed to show that he even knew how to smile.

But he had never truly known despair until he saw the People Taker stuff Fernie in his sack, pull the drawstring tight, and strut out the front door of the Too Much Sitting Room.

He hadn't known despair until he heard Fernie crying his name, ordering him not to even dare think that any of this was his fault.

Gustav wasn't sad that he was now stuck to this chair, *part of* this chair, forever.

He wasn't sad that anybody who entered this room from now until the end of time would always find him, still sitting where he was now.

He wasn't even sad that there was no escape

from this predicament, not from now until the very end of the world.

There would be plenty of time to be sad about those things; enough time to forget that he ever was a boy who could get up, walk around, have adventures, and sometimes even go out into the yard and talk to other people.

But right now he couldn't be sad about any of that. He could be sad only about a girl he'd just met for the first time the previous day, who had crossed the street, talked to him, invited him back across the street to meet her family, punched him in the shoulder, called his house stupid, hugged him, and called him a friend, and who had been so kind and brave that she'd taken time to worry about him being sad even as she was being stuffed in a sack and carried away to be thrown in the Pit for Lord Obsidian.

He hadn't really had time to tell her much about himself: not what had happened to his real parents, not how he'd come to live with shadows, not what would happen to him if he ever took one step outside his front yard. He would never be able to show her the fun parts of his house like the carousel or the arcade or even his favorite place, the Planetarium of the Neverworlds.

Nor would he ever have a chance to learn about the world she came from, about what her father was like and what her mother was like and what her sister was like and even what her stupid cat was like. He had wanted to ask her what it had been like to go to school and to walk around under the sun and have people around her who she could touch and talk to and hug as much as she wanted. Most of all, he wished he could ask her what it was like to live a life so special that even when she was being stuffed in a sack by the People Taker, she still had enough room in her heart to worry about how sad this would leave a boy she'd known for less than a day.

That all made Gustav sadder than he'd ever been, sadder than he'd ever known he could be. It made him so sad, in fact, that something happened to him that had not happened to him in years.

He began to cry.

The room blurred. His eyes burned. His tears welled over and streamed down his cheeks in waves. His nose stuffed up and began to run. He shook his head and wiped his face dry with the back of his jacket sleeve and . . .

. . . and . . .

"Wait a minute," Gustav said.

He studied his right arm, which he'd just used to wipe his face. Doing that had required him to lift it off the armrest. The armrest that his arm was now supposed to be *part* of.

He put his arm back down on the armrest and then immediately picked it up again. He had no trouble moving it. Nor did he have any trouble moving his left arm. Nor, he discovered, did he have any trouble standing up.

"That's interesting," Gustav said.

He looked down at the chair he had just left. It looked exactly like all the other chairs in the room. It *was*, he knew, exactly like all the other chairs . . . and it should have trapped him in its eternal grip. Except that it hadn't.

"I can stand," he told the room. "I can *walk*."

Two dozen people trapped in just as many chairs all shouted at him in just as many languages, all of them calling him their version of the name an English speaker called him. "Showoff!"

Gustav supposed that bragging about his personal miracle in the presence of all those people who were still trapped in their chairs had been a rude thing to do. "Sorry. I'm just surprised. This isn't supposed to happen."

"So it's not supposed to happen," one of the trapped figures growled. "We all know it's *not supposed to happen*, and we all know that it *happened, anyway*. I'm sure you can find out why later on. Right now, why don't you go do something useful with yourself other than stand there bragging? Like, gee, I don't know . . . *saving that poor girl*?"

For a man who'd been stuck in an easy chair for the last few centuries, the fellow really did have a way of getting to the heart of a problem.

"Thank you," Gustav said.

"Don't waste time thanking me," the trapped man snapped. "Just go!"

Gustav went.

He raced out the door and into the stairwell, taking the steps three at a time and hitting the first landing so fast that he turned himself around by grabbing the railing and swinging himself around like the end of a whip. He took the next set of steps four at a time, wishing that he were like one of his many shadow siblings who, when in a hurry, did not so much run as glide.

He ran thinking of Fernie and how she might be plunging helplessly into the Pit even now.

He threw open the door at the top of the stairs thinking of how he wouldn't let that be true, how the People Taker might have taken his own sweet time carrying her there, and how there were any number of things that could have delayed them.

He burst out into the grand parlor, which was as always teeming with uncounted thousands of dark shapes drifting to and fro on their various mysterious errands. He ran around the grand staircase and toward the opposite wall, heading toward one particular passage out of many, as it was the fastest way to get to the Pit, and hating how far away it was.

His only hope was to get to the Pit as quickly as he could, get to Fernie if she hadn't been thrown in yet, and somehow keep the People Taker busy enough for Fernie to run away. He knew that if he could not defeat the People Taker, the most he might be able to give Fernie was a one-minute head start. Gustav wasn't about to give up even if that minute was the best he could do, but it really would have been nice to work out something more permanent.

He ran toward the corridor that would take him to the secret passage that would take him to the trapdoor that was the fastest possible way to the room where his new friend Fernie had probably already been thrown into the Pit. Then, all of a sudden, he heard a rich, worried voice way on the other side of the parlor, calling, "Hello!?!? Mr. Gloom?"

Gustav recognized the voice. He had heard it once before, when the man who owned it had been standing across the street listening to Mrs. Everwiner's story about the rude cashier.

A girl said, "This house has *ghosts*! Why couldn't we live here?"

Her voice sounded so much like Fernie's, only older, that Gustav's heart suffered a pang at the thought that he might not have his new friend Fernie any longer.

Already knowing what he was about to see and how much it would complicate his problems, Gustav turned toward the source of the voices. Fernie's father and older sister stood at the entrance to the grand parlor, gaping at the sights they had found inside the Gloom household.

The man seemed one step away from panic. The girl seemed incapable of considering that there might be reason for any.

Neither one spotted Gustav right away

because he was on the opposite side of the parlor and there were too many overlapping shadows wandering about between them. They didn't notice when Gustav, doing what he knew Fernie would have wanted him to do, turned his back on his only chance to rescue her and started running toward them instead in order to warn them away before they wandered into more trouble.

But as Gustav started to run toward them, the People Taker emerged from one of the side hallways to stride across the room with a big friendly and utterly lying grin on his face.

For some reason Gustav didn't know, the People Taker had disguised himself. He no longer wore the short cape or the crooked top hat. He had changed into a white T-shirt and a pair of shorts as well as a chef's hat and a white apron bearing the words PANCAKE CHEF. To Gustav, who knew him, the apron just made him a menacing killer who happened to be wearing a chef's hat and an apron that said PANCAKE CHEF. But the getup already seemed enough to reassure Mr. What, who strolled toward him extending a friendly hand. "Hi! You must be Brad!"

Gustav could already tell that he wouldn't

reach the Whats before the People Taker did.

But maybe he could still warn them. Maybe he could still impart the danger in words they would believe and get them to run away before it was too late. He threw out his hand and opened his mouth to yell, "No, get away! That's not Brad; that's not anything that could possibly be thought of as a Brad."

But before he could speak, the air before him got impossibly colder and darker, and he knew that he was already far too late.

An inky blackness swept across the floor like an evil wind, taking on the form of a silent whirlwind that rose from the tiles in his path to swallow up all the space between Gustav and the strangers he would have given his life to save. A mouth wide enough to swallow four of him whole and still have room for fries gaped wide, revealing that the familiar monster was even darker on the inside than it was on the outside.

There was no chance of going around it.

There was no chance of getting past it.

And there was no chance of outrunning it.

The Beast had caught up with him.

CHAPTER FIFTEEN
FERNIE WATCHES THE WORST TELEVISION SHOW *EVER*

Depending on the way Fernie What looked at it, the People Taker had been either a really considerate maniac or a very cruel one. He'd left the television set on for her and allowed her to watch her father and sister as they ventured, impressed and apprehensive but determined to be good neighbors, down the long entrance hallway of the Gloom mansion.

Like most characters on television doing something that was about to get them killed, they didn't hear anybody watching them tell them that they were about to be killed.

Like anybody who had ever watched a scary movie, Fernie asked the universe at the top of her lungs, "How could *anybody* be stupid enough to walk into *this* house and walk down *that* hall and not know it's bad news?"

The universe was far too polite to point out

that she'd done the same thing in search of a lost cat just a few hours earlier.

On the screen, her father and sister arrived and stood at the entrance to the main parlor, their eyes wide as they took in all the hundreds, or thousands, of dark shapes milling about in the room before them.

Mr. What's mouth fell open, but his eyes looked busy. Behind them, Fernie knew, sat a brain counting all the unpadded edges, all the sharp places that could be brushed against, all the shadows where loose nails could be hiding. The grand staircase would of course be the worst thing he saw, as staircases were just teeming with possible accidents. To him, the hundreds of ghostly shapes wandering to and fro before his eyes might not have been even nearly as disturbing as all the possible places where a careless person could trip.

Pearlie didn't seem to have made up her mind what to think of the house or all of the strange shapes moving around inside, but from the light beginning to dawn in her eyes, she was about to declare how much she loved it.

Fernie struggled. The unseen noose around her neck pulled her back. She coughed, used her free hand to search her neck for whatever was holding her back, and found nothing. "This is stupid! How can I possibly be tied down with *an invisible rope*?"

"It's not invisible," somebody said.

She whipped her head around and saw her own shadow, which the room's single candle cast against one of the gray walls. Like her, it was trapped in a chair, but unlike her, it was held in place by a dark black line extending from its neck to a ring set in the nearest wall. Also unlike her, it had both hands wrapped around that cord and was yanking at it with all its might.

Fernie remembered the banquet hall. "You ate shadow food for me."

"You were hungry."

Next, Fernie remembered the library. "And you attacked the Beast for me."

Her shadow gave the rope another ineffective tug. "You were in trouble."

Fernie peered at the shadow cord that leashed her shadow self. "The cord isn't around my neck. It's around yours."

Her shadow struggled. "About time you figured it out!"

On the TV screen, Fernie's dad called out

an anxious hello. Beside him, Pearlie declared how much she *loved* this house. The People Taker extended a friendly hand as he strolled across the parlor to say hello. He wore an apron reading PANCAKE CHEF.

This struck Fernie as the worst thing he had done yet. *Taking* people and throwing them into a bottomless pit to become slaves of a guy named Lord Obsidian was evil enough, but promising them pancakes first and not giving them any added an entirely different level of cruelty.

Fernie thrashed, felt the usual yank on her neck as punishment, and in desperation turned to her shadow again. It was still struggling uselessly with the shadow cord.

Fernie cried, "Am I only being held here because you're tied down?"

Pulling at the shadow cord with all the strength it had, the shadow Fernie gasped in pain and exhaustion before falling back in defeat. "Yes!"

"That's not right! I know you can hold me in place for some reason, but you can also separate from me anytime you want! Why won't you let me go so I can leave and try to save my family?"

The shadow Fernie gathered up her strength and attacked the shadow cord again. *"Because I love you and I don't want to be separated from you!"*

Though it was just a dark outline, the shadow Fernie's efforts seemed heroic; Fernie could almost see the straining muscles, the sheen of sweat, the eyes shut tightly in concentration. But it did the shadow Fernie no good. The cord was too strong to be broken that way.

On the TV screen, Fernie's family and the People Taker had a nice chat as he led them across the parlor.

"Don't worry about all this," the People Taker assured them. "None of what you're seeing is really real. I'm a professional special effects man for amusement parks and I was working on something just before Fernie came in. I guess I forgot to turn the projector off before getting started on breakfast! Ha, ha, ha!"

He'd said the actual words *ha, ha, ha*, as his laugh was so chilling, it might have been enough to warn Mr. What that something was terribly wrong.

Mr. What chuckled. "It's pretty impressive work, Brad! You almost fooled me! Me, I'm a safety expert. I make a living out of seeing all the hidden dangers that people don't notice!"

"Really?" The People Taker sounded fascinated. "There much money in that?"

"There is if you're good at it!" Mr. What said. "And I'm the best! No hidden danger ever gets past me ever!"

Fernie had never been the kind of girl who yelled at her dad, not even when he drove her crazy with all his safety talk; but there had been times in her life when she would have liked to, and this was one of those times. As it happened, only the TV set was present, so she yelled at it instead, calling it a big fat dumb stupid-head idiot *safety expert*. When she was done, she whirled to face her shadow again and saw that it was still struggling with the cord around its neck, still wasting time when the People Taker was on the TV leading Fernie's father and sister to the Pit.

Fernie would have given everything she had in the world just for a pair of scissors capable of cutting a shadow cord. If she only had a pair of scissors like that, she could have freed her shadow and talked it into running away with her—maybe even into helping her get back to the Pit before the People Taker did—and finding some way to push *him* into the Pit before he could do the same to her family. Then they could go back to the Too Much Sitting Room and do something, anything, to get poor Gustav out of that chair.

There was no possible way, she thought, to get a pair of scissors while she was as leashed as her shadow and might as well be making shadow pictures on the wall for all the good she could do for herself.

There was no—

Her last thought had just hit a brick wall and bounced back.

She looked at her right hand. She looked at the shadow version of herself, still struggling with the cord. She looked at her hand again.

It couldn't possibly be that simple.

She said, "Hey."

Her shadow said, "What?"

"Go back to doing what I do. Just for a second."

She held her hand up to the flickering light of the candle and made scissoring motions with her index and middle fingers. On the wall where the shadows were cast, it looked just like a child's hand pretending to be a pair of scissors. Fernie moved her hand against the light, then moved her shadow scissors up the wall, against the shadow cord that bound her shadow self.

She closed her index and middle fingers.

The cord snapped.

Freed, the shadow Fernie leaped up, spinning frantically as it tried to figure out what to do.

Also freed, the real Fernie did the same. "You silly whatever you are! Why didn't you just *tell* me I could do that?"

Fernie's shadow glared at her . . . and, for a moment, just like Great-Aunt Mellifluous, didn't look like a shadow at all. It had form and substance and a face, all of which looked just like Fernie's except darker and smokier and more transparent. The only bright parts of it were its eyes, which had so much life in them, so much inner strength and wild energy, that it startled Fernie to realize that they looked just like her own. "Sorry," the shadow Fernie said. "I didn't think of it."

Fernie had to admit that there was something about being captured and tied to a chair that was capable of reducing even shadows to shadows of their usual selves. But there was no time to worry about it now. She whirled around, grabbed the chair by its back, and ran from the room, using the same dark passage the People Taker had used to carry her in.

Her shadow followed her along the stone wall, its outline turning rough and bumpy wherever it was distorted by the uneven stones. "No, Fernie!

Not that way! I have to lead you out of the house!"

Fernie wanted that more than she'd ever wanted the sum total of gifts she'd ever received for all her birthdays, but there was still something she wanted even more. "No, thanks."

"I know how you feel," the shadow Fernie said. "But I'm telling you, you can't stop him. You saw the way he beat Gustav. Even before Lord Obsidian got him, he was stronger and faster and more dangerous than you could ever hope to be, and he came out of the Dark Country with strength that no man should ever be allowed to have. If you get in his way again, you'll just give him another chance to *take* you. It's safer to just let me show you the way out."

"I know," Fernie said, breaking into a run as she reached a flight of stairs she had last traveled as a prisoner under the People Taker's arm.

"You're headed back to the Pit room," Fernie's shadow noted as the real Fernie carried her chair down those steps.

"Yup."

"You know I can stop you," Fernie's shadow said. "I stopped you at the banquet hall and I could stop you now. It would be for your own good."

"So would saving my family."

"You don't even have a plan. Please. You could get away."

Knowing that she didn't have the time for this conversation but also aware that she could not escape it, Fernie stopped between one step and the next, put the chair down, and pointed an angry finger at her own shadow's face. "Do you really think that would be a happy ending?"

"No. But you could live."

"Yes, I could live. But let me tell you what would become of me if I *lived* after not even trying to save my father and sister. It wouldn't be all bad. My mother would come home from her adventures and take care of me, but as hard as she'd try, I'd never smile again. I'd never make any friends because I wouldn't deserve any. I'd never do anything that was the slightest bit fun because I wouldn't deserve that, either. I'd have nightmares every night for the rest of my life. I'd spend all my free time sitting in dark rooms with all the shades drawn and all the lights off, forever, because wherever there's no light there are no shadows, and as much as I could help it I wouldn't ever want to see any shadow ever again. Especially," she said, jabbing her finger at her shadow, "if you didn't do something to help me save them, *you*. That's how I would *live*. And living that way is *not worth it*."

Fernie said all of that in as close to a single breath as she could, because there wasn't much time left and slowing herself down long enough to breathe could have been the difference between a father and a sister living with her in a Fluorescent Salmon house and a father and a sister lost to the Dark Country.

Her shadow floated before her, looking stunned. Then, after a moment, it said, "Okay."

Fernie thrust her chin out. "Okay *what*?"

"Okay *okay*."

"Are you gonna *help* me?"

"I *said* okay."

"I didn't know what kind of *okay* that was. It could have been some other kind of *okay*."

"No, it meant *okay*. Okay?"

"Okay," Fernie said.

She picked up the chair again and resumed her charge to the rescue, her bemused shadow following close behind. She still didn't have the slightest idea what she was going to do when she saw the People Taker again, but it didn't matter. He was in trouble now.

CHAPTER SIXTEEN
THE BATTLE OF THE SMASHING COUCHES

Seeing before it the boy who had engineered that whole embarrassing business with the Statue of Awkward Liberty, and being, like most of the world's most terrible monsters, excessively concerned with its own dignity, the Beast gathered up all of its impossible strength and resentment at being made to look stupid and attacked.

The first slash of its claws could have sliced a school bus in half.

It was a little surprised when the swing cut nothing but air and didn't end with various pieces of little boy stuck between its claws. That was all right. Every monster is used to fighting the kind of people who insist on fighting monsters and knows that many of them have some surprisingly good moves. The boy had pulled off an impressive dodge, but it was not the kind of thing that even a boy raised by shadows could possibly do more than once. He seemed to recognize that he was doomed. Just look at him: falling to his knees, throwing his arms over his head in what looked like a desperate attempt to protect himself from being crushed like a bug.

There's only one possible answer to that for a self-respecting Beast, and that was to go ahead and crush the boy like a bug.

The Beast thought this was an absolutely terrific idea and would have given itself a medal for it had it ever imagined the giving of awards for rending and tearing. After all, crushing puny boys like bugs was one of its favorite activities. It considered itself very good at it, and given the powers of speech it would have been able to deliver a fine scholarly lecture on all the best ways to smash them into nice, flat puddles.

It curled two of its terrible shapeless hands in a pair of boulder-size fists and brought them down in a mighty hammering blow. The parlor echoed with a terrible crash of splintered tile and powdered stone.

The Beast peered into the crater its fists had made of a section of parlor floor and would have been perfectly satisfied were it not for the absence of any crushed little boys.

It seemed that this kid actually *could* dodge the Beast's blows, which would have been worrisome enough, if not for a more pressing question: Why had the child bothered with all that stuff with falling to his knees and throwing his arms over his head and all but daring the Beast to try to smash that one particular spot if he wasn't going to be considerate and let himself be hit?

The Beast suddenly felt something scrambling up one of its arms.

It was the boy.

The Beast found this extremely annoying, not to mention puzzling, because no flesh-and-blood boy should have been able to climb a creature made of shadow, even if that creature had made itself solid enough to hurt him. It just wasn't in the rules. The Beast had never seen the list of rules, but it knew that there *were* rules and it knew that this broke all of them.

This annoyed the Beast so much that it reached over with one of its many other arms to pluck the little boy off and crush him into chunky boy juice. But by the time the Beast had grabbed for the spot where the boy had been, he had scrambled onto its shoulders. By the time the Beast grabbed for him again, the boy had scrambled farther and was wrapped around the creature's neck. By the time the Beast grabbed at its neck, the boy was past the neck and was riding the top of its head.

The Beast roared with confusion.

In the Beast's experience, flesh-and-blood things couldn't touch shadow things that didn't want to be touched and certainly should not have been able to climb them like a ladder.

A possible answer flitted across the Beast's tiny mind before sinking into the murk of its stupidity. Maybe the boy was somehow neither flesh nor shadow but something *else*, something the Beast had never even heard of, something the Beast had never once paused to consider.

The Beast was still thinking about how ridiculous this was when it felt the first sharp pain on the top of its head. Its next roar was one of distress, and for the first time the Beast began to realize that it might be in serious trouble. It didn't enjoy that idea even one bit.

Gustav hung on to the top of the Beast's massive head, clutching shadow-stuff. The way the Beast was bucking and running around in circles, he needed both hands just to stay put, which meant that as far as pressing his attack was concerned, there was really only one thing he could do.

He took a bite.

Shadows have a taste all their own, and this one tasted a little like the mud at the bottom of a duck pond that's never been dredged.

The Beast cried out in pain and grabbed for him again. Gustav scrambled down the Beast's spine to that annoying place in the center of everybody's back that no one can ever scratch unless they have a long stick or a very good friend.

He took another bite.

Now thoroughly indignant, the Beast spun around two or three times to look for some way of dealing with this annoyance and then picked up one of the parlor's many dusty couches in one of its hands and tried to use it as a flyswatter. By this time, Gustav was no longer on its back but had climbed back to the top of its head.

The Beast smacked itself over the head with the couch.

The couch broke in half.

Gustav had seen the dusty old antique being swung in his direction and dropped down over the creature's sloping forehead. He rode the narrow strip of darkness between what should have been the eyes, remaining there even as the wreckage of the couch plummeted past him.

The Beast roared in frustration and rage and cast about for more things to hit itself with. It found another couch, this one plucked from a conversation pit where a dozen shadows in elegant dress had been sitting together and enjoying fond memories of their latest trip to Liechtenstein. The shadows dove for safety as the Beast seized their couch and whomped itself over the head hard enough to reduce the poor antique to dust.

It didn't notice that Gustav had already jumped off and was running as fast as he could.

He was halfway to the corridor where the People Taker had escorted Fernie's father and sister when he heard more smashing furniture behind him. He could tell that he'd gained only a few seconds. But he didn't care about that. He cared more about something that he hadn't had time to realize until now.

Since the People Taker had returned to the

parlor without Fernie, it almost certainly meant that he was already done with her, that she was probably already plummeting into the Pit and facing a lifetime of slavery at the hands of Lord Obsidian. Her whole life had been ruined just because she'd happened to move in across the street from Gustav Gloom. Her whole life had been destroyed just because Gustav had been content all these months with hiding from the People Taker instead of doing something about him.

It was too late to save her. It would probably be too late to save her family. But it would not be too late to make the People Taker pay.

CHAPTER SEVENTEEN
MR. WHAT KINDLY OFFERS HIS SERVICES

Fernie's dad had always prided himself on his deep understanding of life's many dangers and on his remarkable ability to take in a complicated situation and boil it down to its most important elements. This was, he thought, what made him such a sought-after safety expert.

It was with his vast well of knowledge in the field of personal safety that he stood with his older daughter, Pearlie (who for some reason kept tugging on his arm, whispering "Daaaaaad" with a sudden whiny insistence that was utterly unlike her), and his odd new neighbor Brad Gloom (who for some reason stood grinning at him, his lips growing wider and wider to reveal teeth that were far pointier than they needed to be) in a room that did not look like a kitchen (and was instead a kind of shadowy dungeon, complete with a stone-lined bottomless pit at its center) and asked, "Did we make a wrong turn?"

Brad Gloom's grin was now ear to ear. "No, Mr. What. You have fffffollowed me exactly where I intended to *take* you."

Mr. What adjusted his eyeglasses, studied his neighbor's face for several seconds, then turned to the Pit, and after a few seconds of serious consideration, thought he understood. "I'm certainly not surprised that you showed this to me."

This turned out to be precisely the very last thing Brad Gloom expected to hear. "Oh?"

"Of course," Mr. What said. "Once I told you about my background as a safety expert, you could hardly be expected to do anything else. And you're right. Naturally, you need to put up a safety railing around that thing. And a warning sign. If you want, I'd be happy to help you fix it up after breakfast."

Nothing Mr. What could have said or done gave him and his older daughter a better chance of lasting the next few minutes than the words that had just come out of his mouth. They stopped the People Taker—or Brad Gloom, as Mr. What believed him to be—utterly. "A warning sign? Really? Are you sssssserious?"

"Of course I'm serious," Mr. What said. "I would suggest one that points out this rather serious danger. Otherwise, somebody could fall in and get hurt."

The infinite wonder in Mr. Gloom's eyes as he stood before Mr. What slowly shaking his head was a thing to behold. "Because someone could always wander by my bottomless pit, without warning, down here in my basement."

Mr. What thrust out his chin and declared the most deeply held philosophy of his entire life. "Better safe than sorry."

The People Taker fell silent for ten seconds, then started to laugh.

It was the laugh of somebody who was not just bad but proud of being bad, in the same way that Mr. What was proud of his lifelong support of safety railings. Only a man like Mr. What, for whom safety had always been a matter of what dangers could be predicted and what special padding had to be attached to things to protect people from them, could have failed to sense that he was in the presence of a monster.

But Pearlie sensed it. She swallowed all the nervousness that had been building in her since she first saw the sudden evil in Mr. Gloom's eyes and stepped between her father and the man threatening them. Her voice trembled, but there was more rage and grief in it than fear. "You threw her in there, didn't you?"

Mr. What was shocked by his daughter's impossible rudeness. *"Pearlie!"*

Pearlie ignored her father and focused all her attention on the figure she knew only as Mr. Gloom. Her voice quavered, but behind it was the kind of courage she and Fernie had both inherited from their mother. "You're not a nice man who makes pancakes. You threw my little sister in there. And now you want to throw us in. That's what this is all about. That's the kind of man you are."

Mr. Gloom's smile faded, replaced by a grimace that seemed to drain all the heat from the room. "Yesssss, my dear. That's exactly the kind of man I am."

He moved.

Pearlie had not been raised by shadows and was not nearly as fast as Gustav. She was not able to evade the People Taker. She just barely had time to do the first thing that came to mind, which was to shove her father away as hard as she could, before the bad man could seize her by the throat.

Mr. What tried to regain his balance, but all he managed to do was change the direction of his fall. Instead of toppling through the open doorway behind him, he spun, fell sideways, and hit the stone wall with his head. There was no crunch, but there was a loud *thud*. He sank the rest of the way to the floor, out cold and no doubt having a very nice dream about where everything even the least bit dangerous was corrected by a safety inspector.

The bad man lifted Pearlie off the ground by her neck, her legs kicking and thrashing with a fury that had more to do with sheer indignation than will to survive. His arm was so long that none of her kicks came even close to hitting him, and her punches just brushed his arm without affecting him at all. He let her choke for several seconds before, that evil smile spreading again, he spun on his heels and began to stride toward the Pit with the struggling Pearlie at arm's length.

He was almost to the Pit when the shadow of a little girl flew in through one of the other doorways, flitted through the air, and darted straight at his face. The People Taker had spent too much time hiding out in the Gloom mansion in the day and venturing forth to *take* people at night to be scared by shadows, but this one distracted him at a key moment. He waved his arm to shoo the annoying thing away, flapping Pearlie at it like she was a towel being snapped at an intrusive fly.

The little girl shadow circled around him and then flew at his face a second time as insistent as a moth determined to get at a lightbulb. This time the People Taker recognized the shadow, because he'd used a shadow cord to leash it not all that long ago. His cry of realization was almost delighted. "It's Ffffffernie!"

"No," the real Fernie said from behind him. "It's just my shadow."

In the surprisingly long and rich history of people hitting other people in the back with chairs, there have been a number of more effective swings. A lot of times the chairs were heavier, and the people swinging them were stronger. Fernie was just a young girl and would not have made any list of the top ten. Frankly, she didn't even crack the top hundred.

This is not even close to the same thing as saying that the impact didn't hurt.

The People Taker fell to one knee, dropping far enough for Pearlie to land with her feet on the floor and be able to swallow a quick breath. He stood almost immediately, yanking her off her feet again and resuming his march toward the Pit with her at arm's length. His strides were so long that Fernie had to run after him to keep up.

She swung the chair again.

This time he reached behind him with his free hand and caught her midswing, snatching the chair out of her grasp with an audible *snap*. A quick overhand toss and it plummeted into the Pit. If it hit anything on the way down, even the Pit walls, no sound returned to offer testimony.

"There," he said. "That's better. Don't worry, Fffffernie. I'll be dropping her soon enough. And then you sssssecond. I've changed my mind about your being the one I'll keep. Your fffffather is way too entertaining to give up."

He was now fewer than three steps away from dangling Pearlie over the Pit. Fernie's shadow darted at his face again, and this time became solid enough to strike him a couple of times, but he didn't seem to be bothered or slowed at all. Fernie jumped on the People Taker's back, wrapping her arms around his neck as if the slight addition of her own weight possibly stood any chance of bringing him down. It didn't, as she knew it wouldn't, but she had no ideas left, and doing something, even something that didn't work at all, was better than doing nothing.

Two steps from the Pit now.

One.

Suddenly another tiny form ran into the room and scrambled up the People Taker's back, wrapping his arms around the villain's neck and unbalancing him so much that he actually had to take a single step backward to keep himself from falling over.

"Gustav!" Fernie cried.

It was indeed Gustav, who as far as Fernie knew should have been part of a chair in the Too Much Sitting Room for the rest of his life but was instead running around and free and, most wonderfully, *here*.

Gustav seemed just as surprised and delighted to see Fernie as she was to see him, but it didn't stop him from treating the People Taker's ears like the lids of peanut butter jars that just needed a strong grip and a decisive twist before they'd agree to come off.

They didn't come off, unfortunately, but they did hurt the People Taker even more than being hit in the back with the chair had. He spun in a circle and stumbled away from the Pit, almost completely crossing the room before getting control of himself and managing to stand upright again.

He threw Pearlie away. She sailed across the room, hit the floor, and skidded to a stop at the edge of the Pit, arms and legs flailing. For one terrifying heartbeat she almost rolled in, but then she looked down, straight down, into the infinite darkness below her, and almost levitated away with instinctive fear of the country far below.

Unburdened now, the People Taker spun his arms trying to grab Gustav. But the strange boy had jumped off his shoulders and was not there to be grabbed; he was instead standing just beyond the People Taker's reach, saying, "It isn't going to be that easy."

Ignoring him, the People Taker snarled, ripped Fernie away from his neck, held her at arm's length as she shrieked, and resumed his march back toward the Pit.

Crying out, Gustav jumped on his back again, but all his additional weight accomplished was to drive the People Taker toward the Pit faster. Pearlie lowered her head and charged him with everything that she had, ramming him in the belly and forcing him back half a step. While the People Taker was off balance, Fernie took the opportunity to scramble onto his back.

Fernie's shadow swooped around another time, again flying at the People Taker's face. Angry fingernail scratches appeared on his cheeks. A flurry of movement ended with three children and one angry shadow riding on the People Taker's back and pounding him with everything they had.

It still wasn't enough to stop him. The People Taker was stronger than all of them put together and was still able to march forward, the grin widening on his face as he saw his victory growing closer with every step.

Then yet another shadow flew across the room and wrapped itself around the People Taker's head, crying out in the voice of a being too brave and too formidable to have ever worried about being protected by a safety railing. It pounded the People Taker on the face with its fists, driving him back.

"Let them go!" that new shadow roared in a voice deeper and stronger than any Fernie had heard from the man who still lay out cold by the doorway.

"*Dad!?!?*" Fernie gasped.

"You know better than that, Fernie! I'm not him; I'm just his shadow! But he'd be doing this himself if he could!"

Fernie had always known that her father wanted her safe, but it had never occurred to her that he could fight for her. With his shadow, she dared to hope, they might even have a chance.

But no; the People Taker was so strong that he could force himself forward even with three children and two shadows weighing him down. Groaning from the effort, he gathered up his strength and staggered toward the Pit.

Pearlie's shadow and Gustav's shadow also separated from their people and added their own fury to the battle, punching and hitting the People Taker with a ferocity that might have been too much for any other man. Pearlie's shadow wrapped itself around his ankles and Gustav's shadow concentrated on pounding his nose, both while calling him the kinds of names that even a man who made people disappear for fun might have found more insulting than he deserved.

It slowed him down only a little. He continued carrying them all toward the Pit.

The three children and now four shadows on the People Taker's back did the only thing they possibly could: They started screaming for help. Fernie and Pearlie cried out for their real flesh-and-blood father, who still wasn't moving. Gustav cried out for Great-Aunt Mellifluous, the shadow Mr. Notes, and whomever else he could think of. The shadows in the fight all cried out for any of their kind who might not only be able to hear them but also be inclined to come help.

None of this did any real good. No dark army came running to their rescue.

And then, three steps from the edge, things got even worse.

An inhuman roar from one of the entrances to the room established that the Beast had caught up with Gustav at last, and it so completely filled up the doorway that it resembled a walking wall of darkness.

Fernie screamed. Pearlie saw the Beast for

the very first time and screamed louder. As someone who had already tangled with what they were facing and knew how badly it doomed their chances of defeating the People Taker as well, Gustav might have screamed louder than the two girls put together if he'd had the chance to make a sound, which he didn't. Because that's when a yowling and spitting black-and-white missile with fur standing straight up all over his little body rocketed into the room and launched himself, claws first, at the People Taker.

Harrington landed on the People Taker's face and stuck there, front claws digging into his temples, rear claws digging into his neck, angry mouth biting his nose. The People Taker shrieked but still stumbled the remaining two steps toward the edge of the Pit. Gustav turned what would have been his scream of fear into a shout of urgent command.

"Everybody let go!"

The What sisters dove for the floor. The shadows flew at the ceiling. Gustav remained on the People Taker's back until he knew they were clear, then dove away at the last second, pushing off with one furious kick.

The People Taker teetered with one foot on

and one foot off the edge of the Pit, his arms spinning like pinwheels in a desperate attempt to regain his balance. Harrington registered the vast open space below him and, with a cat's unerring instinct for self-preservation, decided that the rage he felt at this guy who'd threatened his people was not quite worth sticking around for the full plunge. He leaped straight up, his back curled in a feline arc.

His leap provided the last fatal nudge.

The People Taker screamed and spun his arms but fell in, his splash into the shadow-stuff sending clouds of darkness puffing into the air around him.

The Beast saw its master plunge into the Pit, let out its own inhuman cry of grief and rage, and also charged, a billowing, shapeless darkness afraid of losing what might have been the only being in two worlds it could possibly ever obey. The wind it made as it passed over the prone children felt like a hurricane, if any hurricane wind could be not just powerful and destructive but also downright malicious. Caught up in the wind, the What girls each slid a couple of feet closer to the edge before hugging the floor tighter and managing to hold on.

The Beast cleared the backs of Gustav and the two What girls and plunged into the Pit, looking like a cloud of black exhaust being sucked back into a hole. The very last of it disappeared just as the yowling Harrington, who had leaped straight up and not off in some other direction as he'd intended to, plummeted back down toward the Pit, thrashing all four legs as if he could somehow turn the air to water and swim the distance to safety.

He didn't quite make it to solid ground.

Just as Harrington was about to be swallowed by the shadowy blackness, Gustav, who'd hurled himself toward the edge and made a wild grab over the side, pulled him back up by the scruff.

"Nice cat," he murmured, scratching him on the top of the head.

"Tell me about it," the trembling Fernie said. "I'm never calling him *stupid cat* again. He is *so* getting extra noogums today."

Harrington purred. The shadow Harrington, which had joined him on that last charge and was now beside him duplicating his movements as it had been for all of his life, made no sound but seemed just as pleased with this most recent development as the real cat was. Just what had transpired between real cat and shadow cat during the long night was something that neither of them seemed inclined to explain, but they had certainly come to some kind of understanding.

Fernie glanced at Pearlie, who was sitting up and just starting to realize that she still didn't understand anything that had happened. Mussed by the wind, the hair on the heads of both sisters stood up almost as straight as Gustav's. They both glanced at their father, who still lay unconscious in the corner, a slight smile on his lips the only indication that he might have sensed everything was all right.

Gustav released Harrington, who stretched, licked a paw, and hopped into Fernie's lap.

"See?" Gustav said. "I told you I'd find your cat."

Fernie didn't have a laugh in her, not quite yet. She coughed, spit out dust, and told her sister, "Pearlie, this is Gustav. He's *by far* the coolest friend I've ever had."

Shaking her head, Pearlie managed a breathless, "Really, I got that."

"Gustav," Fernie continued, "this is my sister, Pearlie. She's *by far* the coolest older sister I've ever had."

Gustav looked equally dazed. "I got that, too. Hi, Pearlie."

Pearlie said, "Hi, Gustav."

All three nodded at one another and then collapsed on their backs.

EPILOGUE
CHOCOLATE CHIPS ON SUNNYSIDE TERRACE

The next day, Fernie What sat on the stoop of her Fluorescent Salmon house and watched the shadows dance. It was a bright, sunny day, so the shadows were easy to spot if you knew where to look for them. In the tiny patches of mixed darkness and light formed by the leaves of every tree on Sunnyside Terrace, there were a number of other shapes amusing themselves with games of tag.

From time to time, one of the shadows would dart back across the street to the constant gray murk of the Gloom yard or from the Gloom yard on other mysterious errands.

Gustav had told her that shadows had always been this open about their activities and this easy to spot, not just here but everywhere they lived. It was, he said, just the kind of thing flesh-and-blood people overlooked until they really saw it for the first time, at which point they never stopped seeing it.

Fernie found that she didn't mind. In her book, anything that made life more interesting was a good thing.

Mr. What came out dressed in an old pair of jeans and one of his favorite T-shirts, one displaying a list of instructions on what people should do if they're ever attacked by a bear. He carried two glasses of ice water and handed one to Fernie as he sat beside her.

She sipped. "Thanks, Dad."

"I wanted to make sure again that you're okay."

"I'm fine."

"You sure?"

"I'm sure, Dad. I really am."

He didn't seem to have heard her. "Because if you're not okay, I'm serious about what I said. We can always find another house in another neighborhood. Somewhere safer."

Fernie had been sitting here thinking about what to tell her father if he said that to her again as he had at least a hundred times since their safe departure from the Gloom house. "I know you only say that because you love us."

Mr. What suddenly found his glass of water very interesting. He hid his eyes, but it was too late; Fernie had already seen them go shiny. That had happened a lot in the last twenty-four hours. He said, "But for you to look out the window every day and see *that house* right there and be reminded of everything bad that happened . . ."

"I'm also reminded of the good things," Fernie said. "I met Gustav there. And his great-aunt Mellifluous, who was also very nice. And there's a library with every book that people never got around to writing and a sculpture gallery filled with some of the craziest statues you ever saw. I had fun there, in between all the scary parts. If you ever let me, I'd go back in a second."

His eyes darkened. "And that's exactly why we need to move, Fernie. It's not safe."

She measured her next words carefully. "But that's the point, Dad. The world doesn't have any safe places."

He looked stricken. "Oh, honey . . ."

"No, it's okay. I'm not saying it just because I had a scary night. I've seen your books. Some places have earthquakes. Others have hurricanes or avalanches or forest fires or wars. You told me once how we couldn't ever go to New York City because somebody's air conditioner could fall out an apartment window and onto our heads or to Hawaii because they have volcanoes. It seems to me that every place has something, Dad. We just moved to a place that has one of the stranger things."

"But, Fernie . . . ," he whined.

"I know. You're the dad in this family and that means you get to decide whether we leave or stay. But I just need to say, I think people always have to decide what dangers they're willing to live near in order to also live near the people they care about. And I care about Gustav. I think he's a good kid, and I don't think he deserves to be lonely. I don't want to move away and not be his friend anymore."

Mr. What looked away from her and toward the black house across the street. His eyes grew distant and sad in a way that Fernie had never seen. He might have been thinking about anything, but she was pretty sure he was thinking about what had happened after the defeat of the People Taker.

Gustav had escorted the What family all the way to the front gate and then stayed behind as they stepped off his property and back into the sunlight.

Mr. What had done something surprising then. He'd turned around and begged Gustav to go with them. He'd said that living in a dusty, dark old house with nothing but shadows for company and any number of dangers to worry about was no way for a young boy to grow up. He'd said that if Gustav followed them across the street, he could stay with them for as long as he wanted.

Fernie had never been prouder of her father in her entire life.

But then Gustav had shown them all why this could never be. He'd stuck his hand through the gap between the iron bars of his front gate and into direct sunlight. His flesh had started to smoke and burn, boiling away with an angry hiss. By the time he withdrew his hand back into the perpetual overcast on his side of the gate, his skin oozed with blisters.

"I'm not a shadow," Gustav explained with the same spooky calm he used to explain everything. "But I'm not really a flesh-and-blood person, either. That's why I was able to leave the Too Much Sitting Room. I didn't know it, but the chairs there only capture *people*."

Fernie and her family had stared at Gustav's hand, watching as the gray mist that covered the Gloom yard rose from the ground, swirled around his hand, and became part of it, instantly repairing the damage the sunlight had done.

Pearlie had murmured a soft, "But what are you then?"

Gustav had shrugged, and for just a moment looked like he'd always looked to all the other neighbors on Sunnyside Terrace: like the saddest little boy in the world.

He'd said, "I'm not sure," and walked away, darkness rising up like a curtain to shroud him until he was gone and the yard was empty.

There were still a number of questions that Fernie hadn't had a chance to ask him. She wanted to know who Gustav's real parents were, how he had come to be adopted by the shadows of the Gloom mansion, and just what his childhood had been like if he'd never been with anybody who could hug him. She also wanted to tell him that everything would be all right but wasn't sure that was true. There were things she hadn't told him yet, things that made her suspect that the danger wasn't really over.

The People Taker had told her that falls into the Pit weren't fatal, and there was nothing she could think of, based on everything she had learned, that could ever stop this evil shadow, Lord Obsidian, from just sending him back to the world of light to try again.

The front door opened, and Pearlie stepped out carrying a bowl wrapped in aluminum foil. "That cat," she said, shaking her head.

"What's he doing?" Fernie wanted to know.

"What else would he be doing? He's chasing his new best friend, his shadow, around the living room. And then it's chasing him. They're getting along just fine now. They're nutsy-kooky, the two of them. I guess we're stuck with both of them."

"I guess it's not all we're stuck with," Mr. What said with a sigh, unhappy about living across the street from such a strange house but surrendering to the will of his daughters. He looked at Fernie and Pearlie. "Are we ready to do this?"

"Yup," said Fernie.

Mr. What took one hand of each of his daughters and walked with them to the street, stopping at the curb to look left, right, and—just in case of any airplanes coming in for emergency landings—up. They opened the front gate of the Gloom yard and strolled past the clutching hand of a tree and the gamboling tufts of smoke that could be the shadows of dogs or cats or people or stranger things. They knocked on the front door and waited there until it opened and the shadows gathered in the front hall.

"We'd like to talk to Gustav," Mr. What told the shadows politely.

The doors closed, and a short time passed before they opened again, this time with Gustav Gloom behind them. He was dressed in another jet-black suit with another jet-black tie, and his hair still stood straight up, though it was so shiny that it must have been, somehow, recently washed.

He seemed surprised to see them. "I thought you'd move away."

"Don't be stupid," Fernie said, quickly putting an end to that. "We brought you a gift."

He glanced at Mr. What and at the bowl

Pearlie carried before turning his gaze back to Fernie. "What is it?"

"You told me something the last time I visited," Fernie said. "You said that your family can't go shopping, so there's no real food anywhere in your house. You said that's why your shadow always eats for you."

"Yes."

"You also said that you've lived here as long as you can remember."

"Yes."

"So I put that all together and it seems that you've never really had anything to eat, not without your shadow's help, for as long as you've lived."

"It's not like I ever go hungry," Gustav said defensively.

"I know that. But you don't get to enjoy food, either. I know, because my shadow ate for me while I was there and I didn't get to taste even a bit of it. So we're going to start bringing you some treats to enjoy. Pearlie made you some chocolate chip cookies. Here they are. Try one."

Pearlie peeled back the aluminum foil, revealing a mound of freshly baked chocolate chip cookies.

"Go ahead," she said. "They're for you."

Gustav Gloom's eyes darted from Mr. What to the two sisters to the bowl of unfamiliar but tempting treats. He looked dubious. At last, with the air of a boy who forces himself to taste something only because he has to be polite, he reached into the bowl . . . and pulled his hand back without a cookie. "They're warm."

"They're supposed to be," Fernie said. "They just came out of the oven. Come on. After fighting the People Taker, this is nothing."

Glancing at Fernie again for one last note of reassurance, he reached into the bowl a second time and brought out the smallest cookie in the bunch. He looked at it, sniffed it, again looked like he would have rather been anywhere else doing anything else, and finally put it between his teeth and bit down.

He chewed.

They waited.

And then, for the very first time in the memory of anybody who lived in any of the colorful houses on Sunnyside Terrace, Gustav Gloom smiled.

ACKNOWLEDGMENTS

This book, and the series to come, has only one father but a number of uncles and aunts.

You would not now be seeing it without the persistence of agents extraordinaire Joshua Bilmes and Eddie Schneider of the Jabberwocky Literary Agency; you would not now be reading it in its present form without the input of the members of the South Florida Science Fiction Society writer's workshop, a group that includes Brad Aiken, Dave Dunn, and Chris Negelein; you would not now be enjoying the same experience free of verbal land mines and other clutter without the ace red pen of editor Jordan Hamessley; you would not now be *ooh*ing and *aah*ing over the illustrations without the genius of artist Kristen Margiotta; you would not now be seeing any books from me at all without the patience, love, and constant encouragement of my beautiful wife, Judi B. Castro; you would not now be seeing a human being with my name and my face were it not for my parents, Saby and Joy Castro.

Michael Burstein contributed no input whatsoever to the composition of this volume, but has for years now made regular, inexplicable appearances on the acknowledgment pages of my books. I started this because it makes him yelp in bed and wakes up his wife, Nomi. I'm a strange man.

ADAM-TROY CASTRO has said in interviews that he likes to jump genres and styles and has therefore refused to ever stay in place long enough to permit the unwanted existence of a creature that could be called a "typical" Adam-Troy Castro story. As a result, his short works range from the wild farce of his Vossoff and Nimmitz tales to the grim Nebula nominee "Of a Sweet Slow Dance in the Wake of Temporary Dogs." His twenty prior books include a nonfiction analysis of the Harry Potter phenomenon, four Spider-Man adventures, and three novels about his interstellar murder investigator, Andrea Cort (including a winner of the Philip K. Dick Award, *Emissaries from the Dead*). Adam's other award nominations include eight Nebulas, two Hugos, and three Stokers. Adam lives in Miami with his wife, Judi, and three insane cats named Uma Furman, Meow Farrow, and Harley Quinn.

KRISTEN MARGIOTTA attended the University of Delaware, where she majored in Visual Communications with a concentration in Illustration. Kristen received the Visual Communications Award for Excellence in Illustration, along with another colleague, during her final year at the university. When she graduated in 2005, Kristen began receiving commissions from buyers and selling her paintings. She also began exhibiting at regional galleries and events. In 2009, Kristen illustrated her first children's book, *Better Haunted Homes and Gardens*, and made her southwest gallery debut at the Pop Gallery in New Mexico. She is currently preparing for her first NYC gallery exhibit at the Animazing Gallery, scheduled for December 2012. Besides being an artist and illustrator, Kristen teaches at the Center for the Creative Arts in Yorklyn, Delaware, working with creative and exciting students who enjoy the arts.